Works by S.M. Perlow

Vampires and the Life of Erin Rose

Novels

Choosing a Master

Alone

Lion

Hope

War

Short Stories

Alice Stood Up

—

The Grand Crucible

Novels

Golden Dragons, Gilded Age

—

Other Works

Short Stories

The Girl Who Was Always Single

LION

VAMPIRES AND THE LIFE OF ERIN ROSE

S.M. Perlow

Bealion Publishing

A Bealion Publishing Book

Editor: Lynn O'Dell, Red Adept Editing Services
Cover design: Streetlight Graphics
Formatting: Polgarus Studio

smperlow.com—updates, social media links, and more information about the story

ISBN: 978-0-9992858-2-4

1.0.4-p1

1

The alarm blared overhead. I stood alone in Edmond's basement in a shallow puddle of synthetic blood, staring at my reflection in Ariane's steel coffin. Angling my neck moved the image off the large, slightly raised cross on its lid.

My two top cuspids had grown into short fangs. I ran my tongue over them and a tiny cut formed—and then went away. I'd have to learn not to put so much pressure on the sharp points.

My body appeared to be completely healed. The bruises and breaks from Victoria's attack were gone. My long brown hair was a mess, and my black business suit and white shirt had been stained red, but *I* looked perfect.

I felt incredible. I slid my hands under the coffin, planning to rip it off the stand and throw it against the steel-plated wall for no reason other than to see if I was strong enough.

Hunger roared within me, and I winced. I needed to feed. Human blood could make the pain go away. My mind knew it, and like never before, my whole being cried out with the same message. I had to taste it and feel it run down my throat, then throughout my entire, thirsty body.

Biting someone disgusted me, but only for a fleeting moment. It became a glorious image—my fangs piercing a neck, me sucking down hot blood.

I needed to get out of the basement and away from Eure. I turned and saw the closed door at the top of the metal staircase. My hands went to Edmond's wooden coffin in front of me. The distraction proved impossible to ignore.

I lifted the lid to see the once powerful, headless lord of the Spectavi in his fine, black suit. His pure white hands had turned dull gray.

Damn him! He had loved me? No way.

The crack in the wood at the coffin's edge had expanded significantly from when I had dug my teeth into it. I smiled when I failed to find more than a few small pools of liquid that I hadn't sucked out of the red-stained coffin. I had gotten almost all of his ancient blood. Edmond had robbed me of being Vera, but he was the one whose heart had ceased to beat. In a way, we were even, each having taken one life from the other. The skin of his fifteen-hundred-year-old neck was jagged where his sisters had twisted and ripped off his head.

"Goodbye, Edmond." I gently closed the coffin lid.

Those evil, identical twins were one reason to flee. Victoria was yet another.

I clenched my fists. That German monster had to pay for what she had done to me, and the twins shouldn't be allowed to remain free. But what should I do first?

Why couldn't Kristi still be alive? She would at least have

some idea of how to start. *She* had been the one who dreamed of being a vampire and had spent night after night in their world. Why had Christopher let her die?

I needed to regroup. I decided to go back to my apartment in D.C., about fifteen miles away.

In my bare feet, I walked up the stairs, cracked open the thick door at the top, and peered into Edmond's palatial home. I saw no one, and stepped out onto the wood floor of the brightly lit room that had served as nothing but a long entranceway to the twins' basement prison. Remembering what I had witnessed other vampires do, I told myself to run fast.

In a second, I had moved across the room. Turning back to the doorway confirmed how far I had traveled. I could probably have been even faster had I not been wearing a skirt.

Hunger hit me, like human hunger for food, except more expansive and deeper. It persisted, and I felt it in my stomach, in my chest, approaching my neck, and down to my hips and the top of my legs. The sensation wrapped around to my back. I needed blood.

I grew a little scared, picturing myself drinking from a person. But that *was* the answer. I had chosen to live as a vampire instead of going into the pure, bright light.

Upon close inspection, a slight white tint to my skin was evident. The change wasn't dramatic, and others might not notice it, but it was there and would become more pronounced as I grew older.

My throat became parched. My dry tongue brought no

relief to my chapped lips. Blood was the only cure.

With the alarm still sounding, I made my way through the home cautiously, past all the old art and artifacts. I expected to loathe the sight of them because they were Edmond's, but I couldn't focus on that hatred. My thoughts drifted to Jennifer. It was a little after five a.m., perhaps early enough to find her and drink from her thin neck.

But I shouldn't! I knew that. She was my friend!

My insides ached.

Her warm blood would make the pain go away. A little might be plenty.

I cracked open Edmond's front door. Far to my right, among the white offices and tall streetlights, gunshots came in short and long spurts, then echoed. A Sanguan sped between buildings, followed by Spectavi pursuers in gray. The chase was quite a distance away, and it happened at superhuman speed, but I could see it with my own vampire eyes. Caterine and Ariane had likely freed the Sanguan prisoner. I wondered if they had gotten them all.

I could find Derrick, or someone else to feed on. Maybe it shouldn't be Jennifer, but there were others. What time would the sun rise? I had been at Eure for so long, inside by five thirty every morning, that I wasn't sure. Thinking about daylight didn't cause the same instinctive reaction that blood had, but everyone knew the sun was lethal to vampires.

The night was quiet to my left, so I ran that way. My long hair flowed behind me and settled when I stopped at the nearest building. I had covered hundreds of yards in a matter of seconds.

A military truck with a big gun on its roof approached. I escaped an overhead light by moving farther into the shadows. The truck continued past, in the direction of the battle.

I ran quickly down that street toward an entrance to the campus I had seen while searching for clues months before. I passed two buildings and stopped across from the human quarters, where my room had been.

Roaarrr!

I hadn't made a sound, but the thunderous cry rattled through me. I could clearly picture the hungry lion inside me, as though she were saying, "Erin, I saved your life and gave you the speed that has brought you before this building. Now give me what I need."

I had to go into the building. I would drink from the first person I found and then be on my way. I'd snatch someone from the gym or the cafeteria, dig in my fangs, and taste them. It didn't matter who, even if it were Jennifer.

A silver SUV approached, sending me fleeing back into the darkness. The SUV picked up speed as it headed in the direction of the persistent gunfire.

The chaos was my chance to escape Eure. I glanced again at my old building. I'd have to wait a little longer. I ran down the road where the SUV had come from.

I passed an office building, and then another. Speeding across the long gap that separated two more, a guard booth came into view. I rested behind the last building before the exit and caught my breath.

A gate blocked the road at a gap in a low concrete wall.

One silver SUV was parked on my side of the wall, and another outside. The road beyond grew dark as it cut straight into a thick forest. The area appeared deserted.

I darted ahead, then stopped suddenly. Down a long street to my right, a black helicopter landed. A pale vampire slid open the side door and stepped out of it—William, the Spectavi's chief scientist who I had supposedly worked with as Vera.

Near the helicopter, a vampire in a lab coat held a large silver case. William took it and got back in the chopper, which lifted off while its door slid closed. William had run from Edmond's basement at the sight of the newly released twins. After years of being imprisoned by a concoction that included synthetic blood, the sisters had left me down there to chase after him. What could have been so important that he would risk coming back for it?

The helicopter grew smaller and smaller in the distance. I didn't have time to worry about him. I rushed to the gate and leapt over it so effortlessly that it was like flying through the night. I caught scent of a man in the guard booth as I passed, then landed in stride on the asphalt and resumed sprinting.

I ran faster and faster, my excitement building each second. I was free of that prison. That guard couldn't catch me, if he had even noticed me at all.

My breathing quickened, and the next second, my legs grew heavy—I knew that feeling. Each step grew harder to take, and then I stopped. I had traveled far, but at least at that speed, my stamina had a limit. My apartment was a long way away, and I couldn't sprint forever.

I looked back at Eure. The gray-uniformed guard stared in my direction through binoculars. Over his shoulder, a rifle hung on a black strap. I retreated into the woods. The SUV beside him could get me home, and his blood could calm the pain inside me. After being close enough to smell him, he was unquestionably human.

The man was big and tall. He had to be strong, and I imagined what he would taste like. Edmond's blood had been hot, vampire blood. A human's had to be different.

Hidden among the trees, I approached the guard in small spurts. Leaves rustled and fallen branches cracked, but gunshots from across Eure were louder than those noises. Finally, I rested at the edge of the woods to catch my breath.

The guard must have lost sight of me because he lowered his binoculars and turned toward his booth. My heart pounded. The lion roared.

I sped out of the woods and hit the back of the man's shoulders with my outstretched arms, driving him face down onto the pavement. He tried to move to get up, or knock me off of his back, but my fangs were in his neck before his effort advanced beyond a twitch.

I closed my eyes while my tongue and dry lips grew moist again. Blood ran down the guard's neck. I dug my fangs deeper and had the sense to suck. Luscious liquid flowed into my mouth and down my throat, and the void within me started to fill. I sucked, and gulp after gulp pushed blood through my starving body.

The hunger subsided. Thank God.

Ba-dup.

The guard's heart beat loudly in my mind, like the drumbeat of drops from Edmond's coffin that had called me back to the living.

Fire ignited within me.

Ba-dup.

I drank, the fire rose, and I grew warmer. An intense wave of heat radiated through me. Yes!

Boom!

An explosion sounded from the far side of the campus. I brought my fangs out of the guard's neck and gazed over the gate. Arms flailed at me from below, then the guard tried to push himself upright. The man's job was to keep me prisoner in that fortress of lies. He was huge, and had a pistol and knife to go along with his rifle, but none of that mattered. I had become too strong for him.

I bit into the same spot in his neck. His arms and body relaxed, and when my eyes closed, I remembered the pleasure he must be feeling. For me, the thrilling waves came hotter and more violently. The guard experienced pure joy, shot through his system like a drug.

With a thunderous beat of his heart, his first memory hit me and almost sent me jumping off him. Amidst the heat and flame, I knew his name was Paul, and that he was single. He lived in a studio apartment nearby and drove a white car with over a hundred and fifty thousand miles on it.

I sucked at Paul's neck, and his blood fueled the inferno growing inside me.

Paul was thirty-three years old and didn't mind working

nights and sleeping most of the day, because more than anything else, he longed to be a vampire.

His heartbeat slowed and it took more effort to pull blood from his body. I sucked harder and harder and my fire flared when I did manage to get fresh liquid. Then his heart stopped.

Paul didn't mind forcing people to stay at Eure. To him, it was a job, and the Spectavi had their reasons.

The blood cooled ever so slightly and didn't satisfy me quite the same way.

I slid my fangs out, and the flames within me diminished. I ripped a key ring off his belt and got up. The largest key opened the driver's side door and started the ignition. I took off my suit coat and threw it into the passenger seat, then drove down the dark road, away from Eure, at last.

2

The clock in the SUV read *6:06*, so it was safe for humans to be outside. Two cars drove down the entrance ramp and joined me on the otherwise empty highway. No one seemed to have followed me. Presumably, Eure had bigger things to worry about at the moment.

I had been Vera. I really had. The mystery of *who* had erased my memory, and at least a part of *why* they had done it, had been solved. Damn Edmond. I had been such a fool.

The leather-wrapped steering wheel creaked as my hands gripped it tighter. Oh, to have been the one who had ripped his manipulative head from his cursed body...

With my exit two miles away, I imagined driving to Todd's apartment instead of mine, to an embrace in his human arms. But Edmond had ensured that would never happen. Why had I believed his lies? How could I have been so weak?

I *should* go to Todd's, I realized, and tell him all I had learned about my past and the Spectavi. Even if he still didn't remember me, perhaps he would shed some light on what had happened to him.

By the time I parked on the street a few blocks away from Todd's, the immediate, intense high from the blood had faded, but I continued to feel incredible. Neither too hot nor too cold, I carried my suit coat. A scattering of people were on the sidewalks, and when the first person came near, the prospect of another drink tempted me. The man was lucky I had something else to do before sunrise.

I ran the rest of the way to Todd's. Once through the outer doors of his building, I hit *#-0-3-1* on the keypad to call up to be let all the way in.

Brring... brring... brring... brring... brring. The call disconnected.

I searched the digital directory. *L-o-w-e.* No results. I scrolled through all the last names—nothing. Checking again, more slowly, I found his unit number: *721 – Strickland.* Todd had moved. Or he had been forced to move. If Todd lived with the Spectavi, getting to him would be more complicated. I thought hard about punching through the call box, but in the end, I shoved open the door and left.

I walked the remaining mile and a half to my apartment at regular speed, reminded that I didn't have the electronic fob I needed for my own building. My key, ID, phone, and credit cards had all been confiscated upon my arrival at Eure, and I had forgotten about the fob.

If Kristi were around, I would just go to her place. According to James, Alexander had been responsible for organizing the attack that led to her murder. Unfortunately,

I didn't know where Alexander was or how to get to him. But Christopher? I replayed the night Kristi had been killed, picturing him holding her limp, bloody body.

I grabbed the pole of the parking meter to my right, ripped it out of the ground, and threw it against the building to my left. Why hadn't he protected her? How hard could it have been for a vampire to keep one girl safe? I hated the questions, and I hated the memories. I would find Todd soon, and eventually figure out what to do about the twins, but my revenge would begin with those responsible for my best friend's murder.

Brighter skies had begun advancing over the horizon when I reached my building. Shattering the door was an option, but not exactly a subtle one. I considered driving back out to Virginia, or possibly staying in the SUV. I could probably find an underground parking garage for the day. How dangerous would that be? There wasn't much time to waste deciding.

The elevator opened at the end of the hall. Quickly, I put my coat back on, which covered a lot of the red on my shirt. I turned to face outside and waited. Eventually, the door opened behind me.

A man in a business suit came out with a friendly, "Late night?"

I kept my back to him on my way into the building. "Very late," I called out. I reached the elevator and rode up to the twelfth floor.

It had been over four months since I had walked down that hall to leave for Eure, and it seemed even longer.

Everything had changed. At my door, I placed one hand below the knob and my other above the deadbolt. When I pushed, the cracking of wood wasn't quite as loud as I had feared it would be. I rushed inside and shut the door behind me.

The doorframe was built so that, as I had broken it, nothing would keep the door locked, but from the outside, the frame shouldn't appear damaged unless someone inspected it very closely.

The door stayed closed while I got my sofa from the living room. The parking meter had taken some effort, but lifting the furniture was like lifting a paperback book. I stood with it off the ground and marveled at my new strength.

After placing the sofa against the front door, I deemed it unlikely that a person would accidentally stumble in. That seemed good enough for one night, which was probably as long as I'd remain there.

My apartment was exactly as I had left it—more barren than usual, with half-packed boxes that had never made it to Todd's lying on the counter in my kitchen and on the floor. Dim light crept around the curtains on the far side of the room.

Hisss.

A brand new instinct had provoked the reaction. Picturing sunlight earlier hadn't caused it, but seeing it sure did. Night was ending, and I couldn't dwell once again on the oddity of developing new instincts at the age of twenty-two.

I rushed to my bedroom and immediately shut the

curtains. I threw my suit onto the floor and put on a t-shirt before climbing into bed, completely under the covers.

There I waited, staring up at my sheets, wondering what would happen. At sunrise, would I suddenly fall asleep? When it got a little lighter over the covers, I grew uneasy. I closed my eyes and tried to ignore it.

I failed, and a minute later, my eyes opened. It was definitely growing brighter beyond the comforter. Why wasn't I asleep? I slid to the side of the bed nearest the window and peeked from under the sheets. Light bled around the edges of the curtains.

I shot my body away from the window and rolled off the other side of the bed and under it. My breathing became heavy. How much sunlight could I stand? My back flat on the ground, I lifted the bed with my hands, palms up, and frantically scooted it, keeping myself under it, toward the far corner of my room.

Crak-thunk!

The bed hit the closed closet door on my left and then the wall near my head. Two openings to underneath the bed were covered. The room grew brighter beyond the exposed right and front sides of the bed. I had to hurry.

I reached up on the right, found my three pillows, and brought them down to cover most of the long opening. Then I grabbed the comforter and crawled around with it, carefully pulling it down on both exposed sides of the bed. I folded it over and scrunched it together to make it three or four layers thick.

I breathed a sigh of relief as the last bit of light was

blocked by the comforter, and it became pitch black under the bed. I crawled to where my pillow would have normally been, and rolled on to my back.

Demon!

The word rocked me before my eyes shot open to darkness. I had the sense not to raise my head suddenly and hit the underside of my bed. It had to be night again. Why else would I be awake? I slid over and carefully peeked between two pillows—my entire room was dark. I crawled out and got to my feet. The clock on my nightstand blinked '12:00'—'12:00'—'12:00.' The power must have gone out at some point over the last few months.

I sat down at my desk and turned on my silver laptop. I stretched my neck from side to side. I was a demon. Satan's evil was in me and gave me life. Edmond and Ariane had said something about their brother Nicolas being responsible for the twins' transformation, but there had been no disagreement over the fact that it really was *the* Devil's evil.

The Microsoft Windows melody played, and my desktop flickered into view. The clock in the lower right read, "7:22 p.m." I ran my mouse over the clock—"Thursday September 24, 2009," as expected.

Hunger rumbled softly inside me. Already? It wasn't close to four a.m. yet, when hunting would be legal.

The lion within me stretched, stirring from its slumber. The burden of needing to feed also presented an opportunity. I would go out into the night, select my prey, and have their blood. Maybe I'd pick a young man, alone where nobody would notice if anything happened to him. Or maybe I would risk taking someone off the street. Perhaps I'd choose someone older. Imagining the possibilities made me want it more. There was no way I'd last until four o'clock.

Considering basic logistics, like getting a new license and credit cards, I had a lot to do, but that would all have to wait. I would feed first, and then come back. My internet had apparently been disconnected, but a neighbor's wireless network was accessible. I googled and found that sunrise would be a few minutes before seven o'clock the next morning. That left over eleven hours, plenty of time.

In my bathroom, I turned on the shower and reached in to test the water. It didn't feel cold, just… comfortable. Could I not feel the cold, or was that really its temperature? I gave it a minute to warm up and saw my cross tattoo in the mirror. I pulled my hair back to inspect my neck, the same way I had when I'd woken up not knowing myself. It was peculiar not to see the scar that had been such a huge part of my life. That bite mark had been the sole link to my missing past, and almost as soon as I had learned the truth about Vera, the scar had gone away.

I no longer knew what to think of the cross, because of Caterine and Ariane. The existence of vampires had always perplexed me, and the twins' confirmation of what had corrupted them ushered in a new level of doubt. Why would God have let that evil into the world?

Hot water ran over me in the shower. After the events of

the night before, it felt pretty spectacular. I reached for my shampoo, and it dawned on me that the temperature of the water hadn't been perceptible until it had become warm. Vampires weren't supposed to feel cold air, and water must have been similar.

So much had changed. Another wave of hunger hit me. Such a foreign, unnatural feeling shouldn't have come from my own body.

So much had changed for the better, I reassured myself. I was strong and could do whatever I wanted. I didn't have to fear going outside at night, and was minutes away from picking someone, and tasting them.

Stepping out of the shower, I wrapped myself in a white towel. Everything remained where I had left it. Some of my clothes were packed in boxes on my dresser, and others I had put back in my drawers and closets. I had hated my apartment most of the time, but after living in one room and wearing the same clothes repeatedly at Eure, I appreciated being back.

I rummaged through a box of skirts and shirts on my dresser. At the bottom of the box, a black leather skirt made me pause. Kristi had insisted on the purchase, but I had never worn it. It was shorter than most of my others, and because of the length and the material, I had come very close to returning it. She would have gotten a kick out of me finally wearing it. I sighed.

The dull ache in my stomach deepened considerably. I put down the skirt and found a long white tank top that would come down over my waist. After blow-drying my hair and getting dressed, I added some light makeup. My skin was pale, but otherwise remained very human looking. With my tattoo partially hidden behind my hair, my emerald eyes dominated the vision looking back at me in the mirror.

My black bra was uncharacteristically noticeable under my top, and it excited me to look so different from how I had at Eure. I didn't have to consider if my outfit would draw unwanted attention from men or hungry vampires, and I hoped to never wear a business suit again.

I left my hair down, added silver earrings, and sat on the bed to zip up my favorite, knee-high black boots. Going out so many nights in search of vampires, I had always preferred being even taller than normal. Being able to look a vampire—Sanguan or Spectavi—straight in the eye had served as a small boost of confidence, and I didn't see why that should change.

In my desk drawer, I found my backup electronic fob that would get me into my building later. It was attached to an extra key, but with my door broken, that had no use. I decided to wear my black coat, mostly for somewhere to keep the fob.

On the way out, I stopped in the kitchen at my refrigerator, curious. Inside, I found an unopened bottle of Diet Coke. After pouring a glass, I held it and watched its fizz bubble down before bringing it to my dry lips. The first sip had no taste, like flavorless water. A few bigger gulps brought the same nothingness. My lips became moist, then dried as soon as the liquid was gone. I put down the glass, moved my barricade from the door, and refocused on the drink I could still taste.

I closed the door behind me and watched for a few seconds to be certain it would stay that way. I didn't have to wait long to get on the elevator, and found it empty. Then on the fourth floor, an Indian couple joined me. I stepped back to make room, and they both smiled before turning to face forward. Every inch of me said to lunge, fangs out, and take them, but I fought the urge and kept my mouth shut. The elevator doors closed, and we were alone.

She wore jeans and was significantly shorter than he was. His slacks looked great from my angle. They discussed a movie or restaurant they might go to, but I didn't catch the details. Brown boots reached high up her slender legs. A white dress shirt hugged his narrow waist and broad shoulders, and a pronounced vein ran up from the top of his collar. I imagined her neck's more delicate appearance underneath her straight black hair.

I managed not to cut myself when my tongue brushed over my fangs. What would I do with the bodies? I'd have him first.

The elevator stopped on the ground floor, and the doors opened.

"Have a good night," the woman said, walking out. The man smiled again.

"You, too," I answered. The man hadn't finished turning from me before I spoke, and his expression changed. He caught up to the woman a few feet away and put his arm around her. The pair rushed to cross the lobby and had already reached the doors by the time I stepped out of the elevator.

It felt comfortable outside, which really just meant it wasn't hot. My thirst built over the walk to Chinatown, along the route I used to take daily to my subway for work. My old fears as a human at night were conspicuously absent.

I pictured the bars and clubs full of potential prey. I would choose someone tall. They should be strong and handsome. As far as I knew, any blood would do, but why shouldn't I have whoever's I desired?

A young man wearing a hooded sweatshirt covering big headphones approached on the sidewalk from the other direction. He stopped across the street from me at a red light. I waited as cars passed between us. He bobbed his head and sang to himself. He wasn't exactly what I had in mind.

The light changed, and we headed toward each other in the crosswalk. The man stared blankly, mouthing lyrics to his music, oblivious to the danger in front of him. The opportunity was too good to pass up. I'd have him, and then someone better later.

The light. I stopped and stared up at the streetlight. The cameras. Was one of Todd's cameras watching? Edmond had said Eure was moving forward with their plan to start watching everything, all over D.C., and I didn't know how far the implementation had progressed.

The man passed close enough for me to hear the rap from his headphones. I continued across the street.

Eure must have bigger problems at the moment than wondering what had happened to me, I reassured myself. Besides, Edmond was the one who had wanted me there, and he was dead. Still, perhaps attacking someone on the street before four o'clock was too risky. And maybe Chinatown wasn't the best place to try it. Instead of turning south, I kept going west. Assuming Eure was rolling out the system gradually, it made sense they would start near the Capitol and busiest tourist spots. I began alternating blocks away from those areas, to the northwest.

I contemplated returning to my apartment to search for information online, but surely *somewhere* had to be safe for me. I kept going. Between my disappointment over missing out on my last target and my sheer hunger, I started to feel weak. Waiting until four o'clock was simply not an option.

I passed tall people and short people, skinny people and large people, and every size in between. People of every race and color were out in the city, as usual. Anyone would be fine. Was I overthinking it? Could Eure really have set up the whole system so quickly?

The street opened up to a circle, with a few trees and short grass at it center. Shouting came from halfway around, where a man in a black leather jacket and faded jeans argued at a food truck. With complete clarity that would have been beyond the reach of my human ears, I heard the man claim he had paid with a twenty, while the vendor swore he had given a ten.

I cut through the circle, wondering if a camera on the traffic light a block away had the range to see me.

"Where's my money?" The customer with spiked pink hair waved his fist at the vendor.

"You're lying! Go away before I call the police!" the vendor yelled back.

I focused on the customer. His jacket was almost polished, possibly brand new. A linked chain hung from his neck. Neither matched his sneakers.

"Take your stupid hotdog." The man threw it at the vendor, then pushed a basket of ketchup packets to the ground. He was short and scrawny. He looked like a little jerk.

From thirty feet away, when I concentrated and searched for the sound, I could hear his heart beat softly. As the man walked away from the food truck, I pictured his body being thrashed from side to side between the jaws of the lion. Would anyone miss him?

I took a step toward him, and he stopped in his tracks. He glanced left and right, then turned to me. He cocked his head. "Well, hello there."

I rushed over, grabbed him by the shoulders, and slammed his back into the side of a building outside the circle. I located my next destination and brought him into a dark alley half a block down the street. Holding him against the brick wall, with my cheek against his steel chain, I bit into his neck.

His body went limp. I closed my eyes and sucked. I felt better, stronger, and closer to whole as each delicious gulp traveled down my throat.

Fire swept through me!

BOOM!

A deep beat launched from my core.

I clutched Axel's pleather jacket, dug deeper, and drank on. His real name was Anthony. He was a jerk, or at least had acted like one almost every day for the last few years.

BOOM!

His sometimes girlfriend wouldn't miss him—or she might. He hadn't seen his mother or father for years.

Anthony's blood slowed, then his heart stopped. The blood cooled, perhaps a degree, or even less. I released his body, and it fell to the ground. I wiped my mouth with my coat sleeve, surveyed the street while catching my breath, then peered far into the alley. I hadn't checked as carefully as I should have, but no one else seemed to be nearby. Presumably, I had moved too quickly for the food vendor to have seen me, but had I been caught on camera?

That had been dangerous. I could take the dead body with me, but what would I do with it? If there were active cameras out there, carrying Anthony around would be dumb. I picked him up and found his wallet in his back pocket. His sixty-five dollars could come in handy, and taking the wallet might mean a little longer before the police identified him. I threw his body farther into the alley.

Heading back to my apartment to read about the cameras, I ran somewhere between mortal speed and my fastest. Block after block, I barely avoided all the people and cars. Killing Anthony hadn't gone as expected. I hadn't set out to drink from some scrawny jerk on the street. But I felt so much better. I had *needed* his blood.

I walked the last two blocks to my apartment and rode up in the elevator. With the lightest touch, my broken door swung open, and I blocked it again with my couch. A quick look around left me confident no one had snuck in while I was gone. I laid my coat over the kitchen counter and went to my room.

I crawled onto the bed, rolled onto my back, and closed my eyes. Paul, my first victim, had worked at Eure. Straining deep into my mind produced a memory of his that hinted he had suspected things weren't completely legal there. But the memory was hazy, and I couldn't tell if Paul had really known for sure. But it didn't matter; he had been part of Eure.

Anthony, on the other hand, had nothing to do with them, or the Spectavi, and I had killed him. I had really done it. Was I no better than Christopher?

But what was I supposed to do? I was a vampire. My body *required* blood to survive, and there was no way I would drink the synthetic crap from Eure.

I took a deep breath. God let creatures like me into the world. My whole life had been one tragedy after another, and my transformation was simply the latest one.

But no! It wasn't a tragedy at all. I had power, the power to live in the harsh world and the power to fight back against those who had wronged my friends and me. The blood had been incredible, as it would be next time and the time after that. Kristi's murder had to be avenged, and after all I had been through, why shouldn't I enjoy myself along the way?

I sat up and my opening eyes went to the crucifix on the wall. I drank human blood to live, that was just the way it was.

I brought my laptop over to my bed. Links from Google revealed that Eure's new camera software had only recently been deployed near the Capitol and major monuments. The rollout to the rest of the city had begun earlier that month, and because of customizations required for different locations, would take over a year. Chinatown was scheduled to be one of the first areas to receive the software, and since it wasn't clear if they had gotten it yet, I was glad to have stayed away. According to what I found, I had probably been safe.

My fingerprints could have been a different problem. The police had my prints on file from when I had sought their help two years back. But the Spectavi had explained that, while vampire fingertips kept their unique ridges, they didn't secrete the oils that led to unintentional human prints on most surfaces. What had disappointingly left me with no leads back then came as a relief in my current situation.

Next, I checked my bank account. All of my money was there, over two hundred thousand dollars, because Eure had paid so well. They had probably paid Vera once, but I didn't think I'd ever see that money. I requested replacement debit and credit cards, opting for rush shipping.

Doing that, I realized I needed to restart my mail service. Then, I filled out an online form reporting my driver's license as lost. A new one would also come in the mail.

I browsed for a new phone for a while, and found one that was thinner and lighter than my old one. I didn't expect to be able to buy it until my new credit card arrived, but saw I could pay with an online service linked to my bank account. I would have the phone in a few days.

I didn't bother with replacement cards for my health

insurance or the grocery store rewards program. Deciding against them once again set me to taking inventory of all that had changed. It occurred to me that I hadn't gone to the bathroom since leaving Eure. It was so strange to not be human.

I went to the window and took in the scene that lay beyond it: a low skyline, devoid of any true skyscrapers. Government agency buildings and private offices mixed between museums, embassies, and countless bars and restaurants. The nearby traffic circle had green grass and half-occupied park benches in its center. The darkness.

It was after eleven o'clock, and I hadn't seen the sun in over four months. My last night at Eure, anxious and unable to sleep, I had spent hours thinking about the sun, longing for its warmth. I had assumed I would either see its bright rays during the coming day, or be dead. As it turned out, my nights would be filled with plenty of warmth from within, but I could live forever and never again see the sun.

Forever. That was a long time. I had never dreamed of *forever.*

A silver SUV idled at a stoplight below, and I forced the shock away. I would not be upset or spend all my time dwelling on changes that could not be unchanged or choices that could not be unchosen. I had been lied to, brutally beaten, and drained. Before that, my life had been treated like someone else's property and wiped away at *their* discretion. My weakness had almost doomed me at Eure, and with the busy night begging me to come out, I refused to be weak any longer.

Living in my apartment seemed foolish. If the Spectavi ever did come looking for me, they would find me there immediately. The initial novelty of being home had already worn off, and after I returned for my mail in a few days, that would be it.

I started filling a backpack, thinking that the sixty-five dollars from Anthony would be enough for a hotel room. I had heard of places that catered to vampires, but had never before had reason to visit one. I would start searching for Christopher the next evening.

My laptop fit against the back of the bag, and I packed a few skirts, pants and tops, some underwear and my makeup. I added my black flats, but left my sneakers. I didn't anticipate needing them for a while, and could replace them eventually. My suit coat from Eure still lay on the floor. I definitely didn't want it, but I did retrieve the platinum cross necklace Edmond had given me from the pocket. I threw the jewelry in the front of my backpack.

I decided to go across the Potomac River to Virginia and look for a hotel just outside D.C., where there wouldn't be any of Eure's cameras. At my speed, I could be back in the city almost immediately, whenever I needed to.

I moved my bed and sofa back where they should have been, then considered what people would think if they found my door broken into. I smiled and slid the half-full glass of soda off the counter to the floor where it shattered. I pushed my TV so it was crooked on the stand, and opened all the cabinets, closets, and drawers in the kitchen and bedroom. The packed boxes everywhere might seem odd, but perhaps it would look like a robbery. In any event, that was all the effort I was willing to invest in the ruse.

I put on my coat and, with my backpack on my shoulder, looked over my apartment one last time. Finally, I was leaving for good.

I closed the door behind me and walked down the hall. The elevator was empty, and so was the lobby. I headed out into the night.

3

I estimated that I had been walking for an hour before reaching M Street at the end of Foggy Bottom, with the old streets of Georgetown in front of me. No longer starving, I managed to resist the urges to go after everyone who piqued my interest. When people glanced my way, I glanced back, wondering if they thought me merely a girl, all alone at night, or if they sensed something more. Knowing the truth gave me a rush.

I spotted a few Sanguans, as well. One obviously noticed me and smiled. I grinned back, with my fangs in full sight. I absolutely loved not being scared of him.

None of the police officers paid special attention to me, nor did the Spectavi. When I passed a vampire with clean-cut hair, wearing a neat suit, his scent gave him away. The difference had to be the synthetic blood in his system. His sterile smell served as a reminder that I had thrust myself onto the opposing side of a centuries-old war.

With Key Bridge to Virginia less than a mile away, I began walking slowly on the crowded, cobblestone sidewalk of Georgetown. Groups of people stood around and left only narrow spaces to proceed between the street and the shops that ran from block to block. I waited my turn like everyone else. Most people ignored me, preoccupied with whatever they were doing. Maybe I didn't look so different from them after all.

At a coffee shop just before the bridge, a young man wearing an unbuttoned yellow shirt over a white tee typed away at his laptop. He sat at a bar against a large window, and though facing me, didn't seem to have noticed me stop. His neat brown hair and glasses reminded me of Todd, even if he was a little pudgier. I should keep walking... Or I could go talk to him. The stool next to him was vacant. I could ask him the time, if nothing else.

I walked in and sat down on the stool to his left, then dropped my backpack to the floor. He kept typing.

"Hi," I said. My confidence was an act. I had never been so forward with a guy I didn't know.

He continued pounding on the keyboard for a few seconds before looking up at me. "Hi." He appeared concerned.

"I'm Erin."

"I'm Toby."

"Do you have the time?" I peered over at his screen. "Oh, it's one twenty."

Toby looked back at his screen and grabbed the top, as if he might close it. "Uh, yeah, one twenty."

"What are you working on? It's pretty late for coffee."

Toby stared straight ahead.

"Toby?"

"Sorry." He turned to me. "I haven't had any coffee. I'm

just writing. It's a story I'm writing." He closed the lid. "I have to go." He got up and slid the laptop into his backpack. He left the shop and glanced at me through the window before walking out of sight.

How fun. Aside from the hair, he really wasn't much like Todd. He was likely younger, and behind his glasses, his face wasn't that similar. Nevertheless, that had been drastically more enjoyable than slamming Anthony into a wall and learning his name only when I had drunk him half dry. I wondered what kind of story Toby was writing.

A brown taxi did a U-turn in the middle of the street. Toby sat in the back, possibly headed for Virginia the same way I had been. I hurried to follow him. With my speed and improved vision, it was easy to stay far behind yet not lose the cab. They drove across lamp-lined Key Bridge to Virginia, then headed up a hill and stopped in an area that mixed individual homes, high-rise apartments, and commercial development.

Toby got out, looked around, and went into a diner sandwiched between a Thai restaurant and an Irish bar. I had assumed he'd go home, leaving me with a harder decision to make. While I waited for a minute, my confidence grew and an amusing idea hatched. It would be a long shot, but what was the harm in trying? I took off my coat and went inside.

A long silver bar ran most of the length of the narrow, brightly lit diner. A few customers sat there, and a few were in booths with red cushions across from it. Toby sat in a booth, pulling his laptop out of his backpack. He noticed me and left the computer closed on the table, while watching my deliberate approach. The vinyl cushion of the bench squeaked when I threw my backpack and coat into the booth and sat across from him.

"So, what are you writing?" I asked.

"You followed me here to ask me that?"

"I'm just curious what's so important that you need to write it now, and why you're out so late doing it."

A waitress brought him a soda, took a look at me, then walked away.

Toby moved the glass to the other side of his laptop and focused on it when he answered, "It's a story."

"For what? Are you a writer?"

He gave in and looked at me. "It's a novel I'm writing. It's science fiction."

"So you *are* a writer."

"I guess. I mean, this will be my first book."

"Well that's cool. Congratulations. It's hard to get published, isn't it?"

He blushed. "Well, actually, I'm going to publish it myself, online." Ah ha, he was an indie author. I had read a blog post about the growing trend. Toby continued, "I need to finish this chapter by tomorrow night, that's why I'm still up. I get more work done out of my apartment."

"I see."

"Why are you following me? Should I be worried?"

"You don't seem scared," I lied.

"Hah." His eyes drifted down from mine, to my neck, perhaps to my tattoo. Then they went lower. He shot his gaze back to his soda.

I smiled. "Where do you live?"

"Nearby, why?"

"Do you have a girlfriend?"

He looked back at me. "No."

"Do you have a roommate?"

"No. What does it matter? What do you want?"

Half of me was ecstatic for being bold and walking into that coffee shop in Georgetown. The other half begged me to be even more daring and see my plan to its end. It wasn't as though Toby could hurt me. I tried to look cute. "Well, it might sound strange, but I need a place to stay toni... today."

"You're kidding, right?"

"No."

"Then you think I'm stupid."

"No!" I shifted to pretending to be embarrassed. "It's just... I've been living with another vampire, and I need to get away from him." I lifted my backpack off the seat. "I packed in a hurry and forgot any money to pay for a hotel."

"Why are you running away?"

He believed my story, at least. Maybe I was good at lying. "I've been with him for five years. It was long enough."

Toby shook his head. "I'm not stupid." He peeked at my chest again.

"He won't realize I'm gone until late tomorrow night. And by then, I'll be in North Carolina, or farther. You don't need to worry."

"I'm not scared of him. I'm worried about *you*."

"Really? I wouldn't do anything to you."

Toby blinked.

"I promise. I won't hurt you." I leaned forward. "Please?"

Toby fixated on me. "Just one day?"

"Just one day." I stood up. "C'mon, let's go."

Toby's hand trembled when he took a drink of his soda. He put his laptop away, then dropped a few dollars on the table. He took his backpack and got up.

I listened to his heartbeat as we left the diner. The lion inside me roared.

"After you," Toby said. He didn't seem to have calmed down much on the short walk. His building was new. He lived in a one-bedroom apartment with carpet everywhere I could see except the kitchen. The appliances were modern-looking stainless steel. It wasn't a complete mess, but he couldn't have been expecting company. He followed me inside and locked the door. "Please, make yourself at home."

"Thanks." I couldn't believe he had let me in. It had been hard to resist taking him on the street, and if I hadn't fed earlier, stopping myself might have been impossible. But getting into his apartment would make things a lot easier for me, so I made myself wait the long minutes before completing my hunt. I placed my backpack and coat on the kitchen counter while he walked to his bedroom.

He returned without his shoes on and had become noticeably shorter than me. "Where will you sleep?"

"The couch?" I knew the real answer. "Do you have a blanket? I can sleep under it if it's dark in here."

"Sure, sure." Toby walked back to his bedroom. "I'll be out all day. It'll be dark."

I got to him before he reached his closet. His eyes widened. I held his weightless body close. "You shouldn't have let me in, Toby."

He gulped. "I know." He wrapped his arm around my lower back.

I brought my open mouth down and placed my fangs on his neck. Slowly, I pierced his flesh. Heat and flame ignited within me, and I couldn't keep from finishing the bite hard and drinking fast.

I saw myself through his eyes earlier at the coffee shop. He had wanted the bite from the moment he looked up from his laptop and saw me.

A ball of fire exploded into hundreds of smaller flames. Each landed and began to grow. I drank, and we were both getting what we craved.

He hadn't been able to keep from lusting for me at the diner. He tried and tried to stop looking at me, and was ashamed of himself, but he couldn't help it.

I raised my fangs out of him, and between quick breaths, said, "You've been bitten before. She was beautiful."

Sweat seeped from his pores, and he struggled to gulp. "You are more beautiful."

His hand slid down to the back of my skirt and pulled me tighter to him. I tasted salt on his skin before I bit back into his neck. Hot blood ran over my tongue and pulsed within me once more, fueling each small flame individually.

Pop! Pop!

Pop! Pop!

One by one, the flames burst, each touching a different part of my body. Toby was amazing!

And then the blood cooled. I hadn't noticed his heart stopping. He was dead.

Toby hadn't sought death. He went to the diner instead of home because part of him wished I would follow. He had imagined holding me and had yearned to feel my bite, but death had never entered his dreams. The last vampire had let him live, and Toby had convinced himself that I would do the same.

I lowered his body to the floor and leaned him sitting against the closed closet door. I was a fiend. I had literally sucked the life out of a good man. A human instinct crept up, telling me to feel sick for doing it. But the instinct never really resonated. Physically, I felt wonderful, whole, and ready to take on the entire world.

The lion sat, satisfied.

I found Toby's bathroom and inspected myself in the mirror. My arms, which had always been thin as a human, had become slightly better toned. So had my shoulders. My facial features were absolutely more defined. If people couldn't resist me, then that power was another on top of all I had gained. The symbol of Christ on my neck couldn't hide the fact that I had become a beautiful demon.

I moved Toby's bed against two walls and placed pillows, blankets and sofa cushions over the openings at the bottom. Toby's body remained where I had left it. The story he had concocted for his novel played out in my mind. It might have actually had potential, yet he would never write it. But he shouldn't have invited me up there. It was his fault.

From his apartment, I'd be able to start looking for Christopher.

4

I showered at Toby's the next night, mostly to wash my hair. Turned up as far as it would go, the almost scalding water never burned my skin. I hadn't perspired much, if at all, the night before, and would pay closer attention to see if that was a fluke, or as I suspected, another vampiric change.

I didn't know Toby's Wi-Fi password because Toby hadn't memorized it. If he had written it down somewhere, the trivial memory hadn't stuck with me. I did catch his laptop password, so I used his computer, which was already connected to the internet, instead of mine.

Toby didn't have much going on for a few days, but to be safe, I emailed the people he was supposed to meet, from his account, to cancel their plans. While searching his memories, sometimes only a first or last name, or a nickname came to my mind, but the auto complete of the email website filled in the rest. I would remember that useful trick.

Toby had a little cash, and I considered transferring his savings to my account. My own funds were sufficient for anything I could imagine doing in the near future, but it seemed like a good opportunity to have extra money. Then

I realized doing so would make it pretty obvious who had killed him. No good solution came to me, and he hadn't had a ton of money anyway, so I let the idea go.

While waiting for my hair to get a little drier, I checked for any news about what had happened at Eure. The battle had been explained away as a minor mishap during a training exercise, and numerous stories reported on the plane crash that had killed Edmond. Apparently, even Eure couldn't keep the death of their CEO secret for long. It came as no shock that they were able to run the fake news story. Eure had yet to name a successor.

I googled 'Vera' and got hundreds of millions of results—everything from people, to businesses, to fictional names in songs. 'Vera Rose' cut the results significantly, but none had anything to do with me that I could tell. I searched for missing children named Vera, or anything about someone with that name at Eure, but nothing about a girl who had been raised by Edmond and Victoria came up.

I acknowledged the possibility that Victoria had lied when she revealed that past to me, but since she had been moments from killing me—or at least trying to—I deemed it unlikely. Once again, considering everything else the Spectavi had hidden, I didn't hold out a lot of hope that searching online, with no certain last name, would lead to much.

I tried 'Caterine' and 'Ariane,' but neither brought back useful results. Then I put in 'Sanguan twins' and followed a link to a forum on the kind of disheveled website I had ignored while at Eure. In retrospect, the news on such sites was likely more truthful than Eure's fabrications reported by mainstream outlets. In one thread, someone had a friend who had seen two tall, blond-haired female vampires the night before. The man had stopped at a gas station in Maryland and was headed inside the shop when he noticed the twins feeding on the cashier and a customer at the register. The man fled to his car and drove away. The sighting definitely could have been Caterine and Ariane.

The twins weren't my chief concern at the moment, however, nor was my past. I did hope to learn more about my life as Vera, but that would have to wait. I was headed back near Chinatown to Night, the vampire club, to see if Stan could point me in the direction of Christopher. I put on a dark gray skirt, a black top with short sleeves, and the same boots I'd worn the previous night. Toby's keys and my cash fit in my coat pocket.

I started to put on the Goth makeup I had always worn to clubs in order to fit in, but stopped when it seemed pointless.

———————————

My assumption had been, since I had fed on Toby late the night before, and didn't wake up starving, I would be fine going straight to Night. Walking into the small room, holding my coat, I began to doubt the merits of the strategy. It was like walking into a restaurant, or a buffet.

The dance music pounded as loudly as ever, and the old décor had only gotten a few months older. Aside from that, all I could think about were the young men and women, chatting excitedly in the darkness and dancing in the back under bursts of a strobe light.

Standing, sitting, drinking, dancing—blood surrounded me. A shirtless man came near, and the ache in my stomach returned. The man disappeared into the crowd.

In addition to their tight and generally enticing attire, the patrons hadn't skipped *their* dark makeup. I found myself wondering how many of them only wore it when trolling for vampires, and which of them were Goth to the core, every day and every night. What would someone with such dark blood and dark memories taste like?

To the left of the dance floor was the bathroom where Snake had broken my fingers. I closed my eyes to collect myself and remember that I shouldn't kill anyone at the club. At the least, I should take them somewhere else, and even that might be risky. I assured myself that there were plenty of Goths in plenty of other places for me to bite.

Stan was behind the bar to my left, as I had hoped. There were no open stools, so I went to the end and waited for him to notice me. His statue of Baphomet rested behind the vodka bottles, where it had been before. The symbol of Satan must have dominated Stan's thoughts as a young vampire. He obviously still had some attachment to it, more than fifty years later.

I gazed out over the dance floor and found most of the girls lost in the music, in love with what they were doing, just as Kristi had been. Most of the boys were, as well. Watching them made it impossible to ignore my hunger. I needed their blood.

"Erin, hello," Stan called, walking over in black pants and a tight black t-shirt. He grabbed a wine glass on his way, then looked up at me and stopped. He smiled and put down the glass. "No merlot for you, I don't think."

I couldn't help a wide grin. "Nope." Oh, my God, I hadn't realized how thrilling being back there would be. First, instead of carefully checking my surroundings for threats, or situations best avoided, I had surveyed the scene for prospective prey. I didn't have to worry if it was safe to talk to a Sanguan. I didn't have to be home by four o'clock.

"So, what brings you in here?" Stan asked. "Just come back to say hello? Are you here to dance? See anyone you like?"

I wanted to dance more than ever before. I would hold someone close enough to hear his heart thunder over the beats of the music. My fangs would touch his neck and then pierce his flesh. Oh it would be so amazing! I forced the train of thought to stop; I would get to all that, but it wasn't why I had come. "No, no dancing for me tonight. I'm here about Kristi, my friend."

"I remember her. How is she?" Stan asked.

I pictured her dead body, covered with vampire bites. "She was murdered a few months ago." Damn Christopher!

Stan became serious and crossed his arms. "That's awful. I'm sorry. What happened?"

I carefully chose what to tell him. "A vampire did it. It had to be a Sanguan. She was dead when the police got there."

"That's terrible."

"Yeah, it is. And actually, the reason I'm here is that I was hoping to talk to the Sanguan she was seeing at the time. Christopher."

Stan looked uneasy. "You think he did it?"

Yes. Well, he should have kept it from happening. "I don't know. Do you know him?"

"I know him. I saw them in here together a few times. They both seemed really happy, to be honest."

"Do you know where to find him?"

Stan was no dope. "I've seen this script before, Erin. A new vampire wants revenge for what other vampires did before they were changed. It usually doesn't end well for the younger of the immortals."

He didn't know how strong Edmond's blood had made me. Edmond hadn't been the oldest vampire in the world, but he had to have been close. "I just want to see if he knows anything. The police were so useless." It dawned on me that *I* didn't actually know how strong Edmond's blood had made me.

Stan wasn't convinced, so I pushed harder. "She was my only real friend. She was all I had."

"I know a few places you might find him, but you'd better be careful. Christopher's no weakling; I'm serious about that. And hey, let me go with you to look for him one night I'm off work."

"That's all right, but thank you. I'll be fine alone, and I'll be careful. I promise." It was a genuinely sweet offer, and as someone with no friends, I appreciated it more than he knew, but Stan would only get in the way.

43

He listed a few of the clubs where Christopher might go. Stan had even seen him in Night recently, with another girl. It hurt when he said that. Christopher apparently had no trouble getting over Kristi.

Stan asked what had happened to me, how I had become a vampire. I told him it didn't have anything to do with Kristi, but that I preferred not discussing it. He didn't prod further.

I walked to the dance floor before leaving, but couldn't stay long. All the flesh filling the darkness drove me crazy.

———————

I would have preferred to start out in search of Christopher immediately, but assumed that without feeding first, someone from one of the clubs would be too tempting to not bite. Reluctantly, I headed back into Virginia.

After I crossed the Fourteenth Street Bridge over the Potomac, a man in a business suit walked on the desolate street near a high-rise apartment. He didn't look like a jerk, and he probably didn't have anything to do with the Spectavi. The stubble on his face suggested he was on his way home from a long day's work, but I didn't want to know anything else about him. I didn't care what his name was; I just needed his blood so I could get on with avenging Kristi's murder. The Pentagon was less than a mile behind me, but what did it matter? I didn't hesitate any longer.

I grabbed him and pulled him under a nearby overpass. He dropped his briefcase when we got there. I didn't give him a chance to yell.

While drinking and growing warm, I urged myself not to care. My emptiness filled in, one delicious slurp at a time.

I didn't want to see his life. It didn't matter that he worked for the federal government.

I drank faster. It was incredible. Craig's blood was incredible!

My fangs dug deeper. I sucked harder and harder.

The liquid at my lips became colder. I relaxed. His heart had stopped.

I peered out from under the overpass, away from the Pentagon, and plotted a course to the river. I ran as fast as possible, carrying his body down the street, around a building to the left, and between a few trees. As Craig slipped into the water, I was excited to have succeeded in blocking most of his memories.

At the first and second clubs back in D.C., plenty of girls reminded me of Kristi. Christopher was at neither. No longer hungry, I could focus on searching for him.

Both places were dark with multiple floors of music alternating between loud beats and pulsing rhythms. Occasionally, soaring vocals found their way among the predominantly electronic songs. I could make out individuals easily near the slightly lit bars and during occasional light flashes on the dance floors. The rest of the time, my vampire eyesight helped. In addition to being able to see farther, my vision adjusted to dark or light surroundings almost immediately.

Tight clothes and bare skin were everywhere. The humans knew how to present themselves to draw a vampire's interest. Immortals were scarce, unmistakable, and got whoever they chose. Over the course of watching three hours of dancing at two different clubs, I only saw a single girl resist a vampire. To his credit, the vampire simply moved on. He must not have been starving. She was a pretty girl.

Everyone else was thrilled at the prospect of meeting a vampire. Men and women were bitten mid-song, held up by those feeding on them. All involved loved it. Most mortals appeared flustered when it ended, but got right back to dancing anyway, as if to convey the message that they were strong and could handle more bites. Kristi had wanted those bites, had gotten them, and had died getting them.

Walking into the third club, I remembered how they had tortured her. They must have drunk from her slowly, taking turns until she was dead. Ahh! I hated thinking about it more each time.

If it had been planned, as James had indicated, it had been planned to provoke a response from the Spectavi, to draw them out to fight. And it couldn't have even gone as intended. Two Spectavi had been killed, but so had more Sanguans. What a waste.

The vampires in the club were exquisite, finely dressed creatures, and they knew what they were doing. The thin female in the short jade dress had arrived alone and wasted no time attracting the gorgeous guy currently fawning over her. The powerful male vampire in a tight burgundy shirt had shown up with an intense-looking woman, who carried herself with strength that rivaled his, until he bit, and she melted.

On the floor above, Christopher danced with a girl in the back. His shaggy blond hair made him hard to miss as soon as I scanned that area. The girl was on the short side and wore big heels to compensate. She had light skin, dark brown hair, and wore a little red skirt. Her breasts pouring out of her tight black top reminded me of Kristi at Night.

I moved to a corner to put plenty of distance between them and myself. Christopher's neat attire, consisting of dark slacks and a gray button-down shirt, juxtaposed his hair. His tall, strong body towered over the little girl. I saw them in glimpses, as people obstructed my view and then moved out of the way. His features were clearly chiseled. He and his partner held each other close. It pained me to think it, but it was obvious why he seemed to have no trouble getting girls into his arms.

Three times, he took the girl's left wrist and slid silver bracelets out of the way to drink. When he bit, her legs crumpled, her eyes shut, and she fell onto Christopher's chest. The two of them might as well have been alone; neither paid attention to anything except each other and the music. The girl was in heaven, just as Kristi had been.

Stan's information had been accurate, and for the first time, I began to scheme specifically about how to make Christopher pay. For an hour, I didn't shift an inch. My legs never got tired, and just as easily as I found it to speed from place to place, I had no trouble standing inhumanly still. If Christopher had looked up from the girl for long, he could have noticed me fixated on them. He never did, and it wasn't until they started to leave that I moved to follow.

A valet brought Christopher's black BMW around to the front. Christopher opened the door for the girl when it arrived, acting like the gentleman Kristi claimed he had been. Every second I watched made me angrier. I followed them for over a mile on foot, until they drove into a parking garage at an apartment north of Dupont Circle.

The next night, I ascended from a club basement in Adams Morgan, after not finding Christopher there. Before doing anything to him, I had decided to get a sense of where he went, and when. If a pattern emerged, or if he associated with other vampires, that would be good to know. If nothing else, I could figure out where to reveal myself to him.

The sidewalk ran in front of an almost unbroken string of restaurants, bars, and clubs, and at a bar a few doors down, I noticed a band playing loud rock. I paused to watch and listen. The crowd inside began jumping as the song grew harder. It became closer to metal than rock, prompting me to resume my trip to the next destination on my search.

Before long, soft notes from a piano stopped me. I didn't expect the slow, soothing vocals, either.

His hope still burns.

I followed sounds of the piano back to the same bar. The crowd that had been so violent a minute earlier, bobbed peacefully and quietly in the small room.

His need still burns.

Two guitarists—one male and one female—played on a stage in the back, while the piano faded to very quiet. The male drummer only nodded his head along with the song. I went in and stayed near the door, focused on the source of the powerful vocals sitting at the piano. The singer's mess of dirty-blond hair reached to his shoulders.

He walked away…

She walked back in.

The song picked up its pace and volume.

Her hope still burns.

The pianist got up from the bench, but kept playing.

Her love still burns!

I stood motionless while he slammed the keys.

Their hope won't die! Their need won't die! Their love won't die!

He held the last note and sang softly.

Their love still burns.

The crowd erupted into screams of approval and raucous applause. The drummer began a new song, the crowd picked up its jumping, and the lead singer moved to the center of the stage. He wrapped his big hands around a standing microphone and sang. A gray t-shirt, darkened with sweat, covered his solid body and the tops of his muscular arms. Leather pants hid powerful legs.

He looked amazing.

He sounded amazing.

He sang. The people moshed. I stared.

For minute after minute, I watched his every move. I don't believe I blinked. Eventually, the song ended, and the crowd went crazy.

The lead singer called to them, "Thank you all! We're Shattered Nights!"

The band walked backstage, out of sight.

I left the bar while the crowd continued to clap and yell. I started again to the second club, stunned. The lead singer was incredible. I had to hear him again. Then, I had to have him. My body said so. I wouldn't wait weeks and months and consider the positives and negatives. I was a vampire, and I would act.

I shook the idea away. I couldn't kill the lead singer of some band. Even though they couldn't be hugely popular, it was too high profile. The band had fans who would demand to know what had happened. I had to focus on Kristi, and killing someone high profile might make that impossible.

Christopher wasn't at the second club, or the third. Memories of the lead singer and his music distracted me at each. I didn't like hard rock. The piano was what had called me back to that bar, and that was the song I remembered over and over. But then, as more of the rest of it replayed, it all started growing on me.

I found Christopher at the last place on my list, and seeing him with another girl, a blonde, returned my focus to the task at hand. The new girl was a bit taller. Her white, thigh-high socks and plaid skirt looked silly, almost as if they were part of a tacky costume. When the two danced, they seemed to be in their own world, and to be each other's entire world. At least for Christopher, that appeared to be a lie.

I wondered if the girls knew about each other, and if

there had been others when Christopher was with Kristi.

The second girl was quite unexpected, and offered another way to get to Christopher. I watched them for a while and schemed before heading back to Toby's.

Christopher spent the next night with the blonde. She wore hardly anything, to an extreme even for a vampire club. I stayed farther back and moved around a little while watching them. They didn't appear to notice me. A few people did, and some were tempting when they came close, but I brushed off their advances.

After the clubs emptied, four o'clock approached and the streets were on their way to doing the same. A couple jogged past me on the sidewalk and up a block before slamming their apartment building door behind them. A girl holding her shoes ran down the other side of the street. An old car came around the corner and stopped just long enough for her to get in.

As I walked past the empty windows, no one but the occasional vampire closing up shop remained. I found myself enjoying the peacefulness of it all, thankful my thirst had been quenched earlier. I sat down on brick steps leading to a small row house. The city had never sounded so quiet.

Vhrrroom!

A pickup truck with a loud muffler raced into view from the left. Three vampires in the back were feeding on a man—and a woman, which became apparent when they got closer. The truck screeched to a halt.

The drained bodies fell limp to the bed, and the lone female vampire called to me, "Want to hop on? We're just getting started!"

I stood up and shook my head.

"Let's go," one of the males said, and they drove away.

Inside the narrow bay window beside me, a white curtain parted, and a man stepped forward, cocking a shotgun. He didn't take aim while standing there, staring at me. I sped away in the opposite direction of the truck.

Two blocks later, I slowed and walked toward Virginia, in no huge hurry. Other vampires were out, and I nodded to those who acknowledged me. The ones who acted wildly or were out in packs seemed best to ignore—not out of fear, I simply didn't want anything to do with them.

Halfway to Toby's, I had already passed two drained, dead men before noticing a middle-aged man, possibly asleep, sitting against a wall. I listened to his heartbeat while cautiously approaching before remembering the pointlessness of the restraint. The smell of whisky intensified with each step. He held a mostly empty bottle in his left hand.

I stopped in front of him, and the lion scanned side to side. The man's shirt had been spilled on and had come halfway untucked, but I couldn't imagine him having nowhere to go before four. The lion roared as she circled. The man was mine. I knelt beside him. If I didn't do it, another vampire surely would.

His eyes remained closed when he flinched. "Wha...?"

I could take him inside somewhere where he'd be safe,

but why should I? Drinking from him would be legal. I could have rushed the man with the shotgun, but I hadn't. There was no reason at all not to have the man in front of me.

I leaned across his body, opened my mouth wide, and bit into his neck.

––––––––––––––

For a few nights, I tried to wait until four to feed, but could never make it. It always proved unbearable to go out looking for Christopher while hungry. I stuck to people on dark streets up and down the Virginia side of the Potomac River. I couldn't keep it up forever, but hoped that moving around would keep me safe until after I had dealt with Christopher and could take the time to be more careful.

Christopher went out with one of the girls every night. He usually alternated between them with a similar routine––two clubs, and then back to a different apartment with each. Christopher never separated from his date for the evening except when the girls went to the restroom.

I guessed that both girls were in their early twenties and that the brown-haired girl might have been slightly older. Her outfits were just a touch more sensible. The blonde had the more obviously energetic personality, and always pushed to stay out as long as possible.

Before seeing them one night, I went to my old building to collect my mail, which included my new credit card, driver's license, and phone. I was fortunate to have gone then because the next night, I woke to missed calls and a voicemail about my apartment having been broken into. When their office was closed, I called back and left a message saying that I was fine and had moved away. I told them that anything in the unit could be thrown away, and that I would not be renewing my lease.

Even when not hungry, shopping for clothes alongside humans felt weird. I looked forward to ordering things online once I settled someplace permanent.

I put Toby's body in a closet. It had started to smell, but I was asleep or out most of the time, so I could ignore it.

According to the manufacturer's website, Toby's refrigerator weighed a little over three-hundred pounds. I had no trouble lifting it a few inches off the ground. To further test my strength, I lifted a small car in his parking garage. The car took greater effort.

5

Shattered Nights, a local band that had started to gain a regular following, had another show in a little over a week. Until then, I would make do with the eight songs and two fan-shot videos available online.

Their lead singer's name was Luke. He was twenty-eight and had fans on all the social networks, so I had been wise not to have taken him after the show. Digging through posts revealed that he was six-foot-two.

His piano served as an interesting hook for blog posts mentioning the band. They described what a hassle it was to move from venue to venue, and how Luke had to keep it in his friend's garage between shows, but wouldn't play without it. Lots of girls went on and on about 'Ember,' the song that featured it. Being unoriginal didn't bother me; I loved the song, too. While the female bassist and Luke had dated, to the delight of his adoring fans, Luke appeared to be single at the moment.

I watched their videos when I awoke each night, and later before sunrise. The blurry recordings made me even more eager to see Luke in person again.

I had come up with a plan for Christopher that wasn't exactly airtight, but the first half was simple, and he wouldn't like it. Following him to club after club had grown monotonous, so that sounded good enough to me. Shattered Nights' hard rock played through Toby's laptop speakers while I got ready.

The woman at the store had shown me how to bunch all of my hair up and fit it under the wig she sold me. I had jet black, shoulder-length hair with long bangs. I made my face solid white and added black lipstick. I wore black jeans with black and white sneakers and a black long-sleeved turtleneck.

I hardly recognized myself in the mirror. I had never disguised myself, and like my little act to lure Toby, the whole process thrilled me.

My heart raced by the time my playlist ended. I hadn't fed yet, but knew whose blood I would taste when I found her.

———————

The girl's red lipstick matched the short dress that clung to her curves. Picturing Kristi in his arms, I had watched him dance with her night after night, but that time was the hardest. The black lace in the dress matched Christopher's black shirt. He held her and bit her wrist while I leaned back against the wall in the corner with my arms crossed— starving.

When he finished, she sprang back, ready for more. A single, thick silver cuff bracelet covered her bite mark. When they left the club, she leaned against Christopher. She had a wide smile on her face when he threw his jacket over her.

As I had hoped, few people or vampires paid attention to me.

———————————

At the second club, I tried to let the pulsing music distract me from my hunger, but I fixated on the girl's silver bracelet, whether Christopher's fangs were at her wrist or not. I hadn't drunk from a girl yet. Would it be any different?

A song ended, Christopher stopped drinking, and the weary girl hardly moved. She perked up enough to smile and say something to him. Then, as I had seen him do many nights before, he handed her a small wallet from his front pocket. Finally.

Christopher headed over to talk to the bartender. I followed the girl downstairs and through the crowd, toward the restrooms—a row of eight, fully enclosed unisex stalls, with five communal sinks across from them. Music played as loudly down there as in the rest of the club, and it was just as dark.

My insides ached. Twenty feet in front of me, my prey was alone, and I didn't want to wait. In less than a second, I could take her and have my glorious drink. What could anybody really do about it? I struggled to stay behind her, clenching my teeth to keep my mouth closed and my fangs hidden.

A girl in blue exited our destination and headed toward us. Then came a boy who I watched closely. I liked his shirt and the way he smelled.

Christopher's girl disappeared around the corner. The same lion that had been distracted so easily by the boy roared. I rushed past a couple making out against the wall on the short stairwell and saw the girl go into a stall. With a burst of additional speed, I reached the stall just before the metal door closed. Neon blue light lit the space. I slammed the door shut behind me.

"Ayyyee!" she screamed, while the music held a long, high note.

I pushed her against the corner away from the toilet and fell on top of her as she hit the floor. Sliding her bracelet up her left arm revealed where Christopher had bitten. Quickly, but carefully, I brought my fangs to the same spots.

"Yyee! Mmm…" Her scream died into a soft moan.

The beats of the music picked up again. Heat swelled inside me.

Christopher had met her the night after Kristi's murder. Bastard! Maybe he didn't care about Ashley, either.

I sucked, and her blood streamed into me and cured my hunger. I sucked harder, and honey splashed into the fire from the sweet-tasting girl.

She longed to be a vampire. She didn't have many friends, but those she did have were jealous of her relationship with Christopher. Sweet Ashley didn't care about them any longer.

I opened my eyes and watched her enjoy my slow sipping of the honey that flowed from her wrist. The pace and power of the music fit both the spectacular fury inside me and the intensifying joy she felt, but not the calm scene I saw. I sipped slower.

At the end of one her soft breaths, a dull chill overpowered the last hint of her delightful flavor. Then, just like Kristi, she was dead.

Ashley hadn't known Christopher was also seeing the blonde.

I used toilet paper to wipe my black lipstick from her wrist. The fang mark had already been a mess from all of Christopher's nights of biting, so it didn't look discernibly different. I found Ashley's cell in her wallet, brought up Christopher's name, and texted, *Something's wrong. I feel sick and dizzy. Did you take too much blood?*

I hit send, dropped the phone near her hand, and exited the stall. A girl at a sink was absorbed in a phone call. I sped past the couple on the stairwell, then moved through the other bodies as quickly as possible without knocking them over. At the club entrance, I waited and, after less than a minute, spied Christopher rushing downstairs in the darkness.

Two blocks away, I leaned against the outside of a bus stop. With my arms crossed, once again, I waited. Christopher's BMW pulled around. The vampire walked out holding Ashley like a sleeping child. Christopher wept. The anguish on his face rivaled that from the night he had let Kristi be killed.

He carefully laid her body in the passenger seat, then got in on the other side. Christopher held the wheel with both hands and rested his head against it. He cried for several minutes before driving away. I wished he had cried for longer.

The next night, I found Christopher with the blonde at the bar of the second place I tried. The small club hadn't gotten crowded yet, so the music blasted onto a mostly empty main floor. Christopher looked upset, and his beige shirt was uncharacteristically wrinkled. It was a satisfying sight, watching her in a shiny silver halter dress, teetering on pointy heels, consoling the big vampire. He either hadn't told her something had gone wrong, or that was her idea of appropriate attire for the circumstances.

She brought her neck close, moved her hair back, and smiled. Christopher leaned toward her and pushed aside one of her gaudy earrings, then stopped. He might have seen security footage and didn't consider Ashley's death his fault, but it didn't matter. Whether he was too upset to drink, or afraid of killing the girl if he did, I could have watched him suffer all night. Unfortunately, I didn't want them to leave, so my fun had to be cut short.

I approached the two of them, looking like myself again in a white top and black pants that came over a new pair of calf-length boots. My three-inch heels were on the narrow side, and my hair was in a ponytail.

"Christopher?" I called over the music when I had gotten close.

They both turned.

"It's Erin. Erin Rose. I was a friend of Kristi's."

He remembered right away. "Yes, I'm sorry for threatening you like that in the apartment. I was… angry about Kristi." He continued to look very upset.

I glanced at my friend's blond replacement and her pink martini on the bar. "You seem to be doing better."

"So do you." He gestured toward the girl. "This is Heather."

"Hi," she said, almost inaudibly.

I fought an urge to show her my fangs and nodded instead. She probably knew what I was. "Can we talk about Kristi?" I asked, turning back to Christopher.

"What about?"

"I have a few questions about what happened, that's all. She was my best friend."

The look on his face gave me the impression that Christopher was in no mood. "Another night? We can talk, but another night."

"Please?" It was easy to let memories of Kristi wash over me until I must have appeared as distressed as Christopher. "I'm leaving D.C. tonight. I have a car waiting for me outside, actually. Just five minutes?"

He glanced at Heather and then back at me. "All right, five minutes."

"Thank you." I scanned left and right, and leaned back to see into a room I had no intention of suggesting. "It's loud here. Can we go up to the roof?"

Christopher took Heather's little hand. "Come with me?"

"Sure," she said.

The door to the roof, three floors above, wasn't alarmed like the sign claimed. Regulars knew that, and I had picked up on it after watching a handful of couples go all the way upstairs and not return for longer than made sense. The three of us headed that way, Heather first, followed by Christopher and me.

We climbed the narrow staircase, and I ran my fingertips over the black walls on both sides while debating my options. Christopher's back was inches from me. While the enclosed space offered a prime opportunity to attack him, Heather would be free to run or scream. If I went after her first, Christopher would have time to react.

Step after step, we climbed. I pictured the lion climbing with us. Ideally, I would split up Heather and Christopher and drink from Heather first. Then I could watch Christopher suffer more before his end. He would know that he had let her die, just like Kristi and Ashley. When Heather reached the top step, I had run out of time.

I reached past Christopher, grabbed Heather's arm, and pulled her toward me against the wall. With all of the strength I could muster, I shoved Christopher at the door. As soon as he flew outside, I pulled the door shut and hooked my right arm through the handle so the inside of my elbow held it closed.

Holding Heather's back to me with my other arm, as she inhaled, poised to scream, I bit into her neck and sucked hard.

Red!

An intense flash left flames in its wake. I drank fast, not knowing how long I had. Heather's blood wasn't sweet, but it tasted hotter than expected. She was angry and filled with hate. Behind me, the door opened a little before I remembered to hold it with my elbow. With Christopher grunting and straining on the other side, I pulled it closed again. My flames shot higher, fueled by Heather's marvelous rage. I forgot my need for haste and savored each violent sip.

Two years before, Heather had married her high school boyfriend, but it hadn't worked out as they had dreamed. She hated him.

Suddenly, it was as if a locomotive engine were attached to the door behind me, tugging to open it with all of its torque and weight. My elbow stayed locked in place, and I pulled back. I drank faster, and blood streamed down my chin as I raced to finish with Heather.

Fire burst, and I saw her grandparents holding her children in Heather's rearview mirror. Her husband had deserted her, and it had been six months since she had left the children and driven to Washington, D.C.

I ripped my fangs out of her, turned her toward me with my free hand, and screamed, "What's wrong with you?"

"I love him," she cried, her face wet with sweat. She yelled over my shoulder, "Christopher!"

The force on the door stopped. "Heather! Hold on!" Christopher yelled back from the other side. He groaned and resumed pulling. I fought it, but the door started to open. I feared my elbow would snap at any moment.

I still held Heather around her waist. "Do you think this is a game?" I had seen her spending Christopher's money each day, shopping for the outfits she wore each night with him. "You'll die with him. Not tonight, but you will die in that world. Do you love your children?"

Her eyes became glossy and went to the ground.

"Do you love Jake and Emily?"

She didn't answer.

"Emily, your baby!" She was less than a year old.

"Yes… yes, I love them so much!"

I let her go. "I'd give anything to remember my mother, but I can't. Do you want your children to grow up that way?"

A tear slid down her cheek. "No."

The door opened further, and I slammed it shut.

"Go back to them. Stop playing this game and go back to your children. Christopher won't be around for you tomorrow anyway."

Heather stepped backward, then turned and ran down the stairs. At the bottom, she looked up at me, before rushing out of sight.

I took my elbow out of the handle and pushed hard on the door. Christopher flew away from it and stumbled as I stepped out on to the roof, where a low wall ran along the edges.

"She has children! Emily is just a baby!" I screamed.

Christopher got to his feet. "She doesn't care about them."

"Yes, she does. And you know it." Christopher had to know it because I knew it. "You ignored it and focused on her anger because you wanted her." I could also still taste her strong feelings for Christopher.

"Why do you care? I didn't kill Kristi. I loved her. More than all the others."

"Sure you did." Moving away from the brick stairwell

entrance, I charged him, unsure of exactly what I'd do. But I had held the door closed, I was stronger than he was and hated him even more than before.

Christopher slid to the right and moved to near where I had been. I charged again. I would try to pin him to the ground and suck his blood.

Christopher moved, but not far, and shoved me as I passed him.

Crunch.

My face and body hit the brick wall at the side of the stairwell entrance. Pain shot out from below my right eye. I turned back to Christopher and wiped my vampire blood from my cheek. The pain lessened and became very dull, then went away completely. I licked the red off my hand, loving what I had become.

Christopher charged me and punched the wall where my head had been. I was twenty feet away when he connected with the brick.

"Alexander's goons killed Kristi, not me," he said.

"You killed her when you took her out that night. You killed her by not being there when your friends tortured her." I charged him a third time. He stood his ground, and his fist met my stomach, shooting me back against the low wall at the side of the roof.

"I didn't know what they had planned." Christopher started walking toward me. "Alexander used me, too."

I got up. It didn't matter what he said. "Then you killed her when you started seeing her. She didn't know what your world was like."

Christopher shook his head.

I pictured my bitten, drained friend. "She didn't know about the evil inside us. She didn't know what compels us to kill."

He kept walking. "I didn't kill her."

"Like you didn't kill Ashley?"

Christopher stopped. "You?"

I smiled. He rushed at me, and I leapt straight up, high over his head, but when I came down, he caught my ankle and slammed me to the roof. The back of my head hit hard, and then my world went dark.

From my neck, I grew hot. The aching pain in my stomach I awoke to each night returned, and then expanded. The void within grew deeper and deeper. Blood. I needed to feed the lion that lay beaten, bleeding, and helpless.

Except I wasn't helpless. Christopher was on top of me, holding me down by the tops of my arms, sucking at my neck. I could feel it, and unlike when being drank from as a human, I could think. I was stronger than he was.

I shot my eyes open and managed to move my arms and get my hands around his biceps. I slowly pushed upward. As his chest inched away from me, I grew wearier and struggled to keep up my effort. He kept sucking, and I feared I had waited too long to fight back.

No! I couldn't let him drain me. With a final push of my arms, his teeth ripped through my flesh, and he was off me.

I held the wound while getting to my feet, then let it go, and launched myself at Christopher. I drove him to the roof, where he landed on his back. Straddling him, I held his arms out wide. My legs wrapped around his and pushed them down. I bit into the tough skin at his neck.

The pain at my neck faded. Like lava oozing into me, the void Christopher had created began to fill. His blood— mixed with my own that he had stolen—burned hot. It was thicker than a human's, and I had to suck harder, but he couldn't stop me from taking it.

Whoosh!

I was ablaze. My breaths came quicker and quicker. I was back in Edmond's basement, taking his hot blood— drinking power.

Christopher got his arms a foot off the ground. I stopped drinking, lifted my head, and slammed the arms back down.

Blood streamed from his neck. He continued to struggle below me. "I didn't kill Kristi."

"Yes you did. Just like you killed Ashley." A wry smile came over me along with an idea. "Just like you killed Heather."

Christopher appeared horrified. "No, I didn't... no."

I bit back into him.

Whoosh!

The fire intensified. None of his memories came to me, but the thick liquid was plenty.

His left leg came off the ground, and I pushed it down with my right. I drank on, and Christopher struggled less. His blood slowed, and he hardly moved. I sucked hard, and nothing came. Trying again brought only air.

I let his arms go, leaned up from him, and tried to catch my breath. The blood had never gotten cold, but Christopher's heart no longer beat.

"Is this you now?" a voice called from behind me.

I leapt to my feet, searching for its source. From the darkness beside the stairwell entrance, a pale face appeared, and then the rest of Zhilan, covered in black.

"Is it?" the thin Chinese vampire asked as she approached. She appeared so young. I had never seen her so angry. "Taunting your victims before you're finished with them? Attacking innocent girls to torture a vampire for a crime he didn't commit?"

Red streams and splotches covered my shirt. My breathing had almost returned to normal. "He didn't keep her safe. He was responsible, and so is Alexander."

She stopped close to me. Her green eyes looked up at mine. "Will you kill him next?"

"Yes."

"You cannot," Zhilan said matter-of-factly. "He is old and powerful. Unlike this one, he knows how to fight."

"*I'm* powerful. Edmond's blood made me powerful."

Zhilan formed the slightest smile. "He is really dead? You saw it?"

"I watched his sisters rip his head from his body, and I drank his blood from his coffin to survive. Victoria almost killed me." I recalled my pivotal refusal to leave Eure with Zhilan. I had been so weak and foolish. "You were right about Eure. It was all lies. I was Vera."

She put her hand on my shoulder. "I know."

I didn't know what to do, or what to feel. Christopher was dead, but I hadn't had a moment to savor it. Suddenly, all that had happened at Eure mattered again. If I had gone with Zhilan that night, I wouldn't be a demon, a murderer. Zhilan had promised to come for me, and she had kept her word. If only I had been stronger, I could have still been a human woman.

I stepped back, and she let me go. I had *become* strong— and decisive. The world was full of demons, and I no longer feared them or it, anymore. If getting there took me being a vampire, so be it. "Where can I find Alexander?"

"You cannot kill him." Zhilan's smile was gone. "Christopher almost killed you. What if he had a gun? Do you know what a silver bullet feels like? How weak you will be as the metal melts inside you and courses through your veins?" I didn't know anything. Zhilan kept going. "What if he had a knife or a sword?"

"I would have been fine."

"Maybe, or maybe you would be dead. Maybe the police or the Spectavi will find out about Toby or one of the others you've killed. You cannot sleep under that boy's bed forever."

She had obviously been following me.

"You are strong, physically," Zhilan said. "Edmond's blood did give you that. But you are not powerful. You are wild. While I find the act unjust, that you managed to best Christopher was impressive. Killing Ashley was not. That you let Heather live gives me hope."

"Hope?"

"Hope for you. Hope that you will not always be like the animal I see here tonight. Come with me, Erin. Let me teach you how to fight and to be in control. Let me teach you how to be a vampire."

It was so obvious she was right. I knew so little. But I couldn't admit it, and picked one word to mount my defense against. "I don't want to be in control."

"Then you will not last long. The Spectavi will kill you, or Alexander will. I doubt you will ever get close enough to Todd to speak to him." Zhilan turned and walked toward the stairs.

Todd had scarcely been in my thoughts the last few nights, but I did have to find him. Christopher's lifeless body validated my assumption; I really was stronger than he had been. Zhilan's assessment was also accurate. He had almost killed me.

I recalled Victoria fighting with Zhilan at Eure, and then the battles in Victoria's arena. I would still be helpless against her and so many other vampires. I needed to learn how to fight.

But I didn't need to put away my rage. Whatever Zhilan taught me would help me have my revenge against Alexander. I would discover what had happened to Todd.

"Wait." I ran to Zhilan's side. "I'm sorry. I could use your help." She nodded, and I followed her past the stairwell. She showed me how to climb down from the roof, and we sped away.

6

"I will be here when you wake up." Zhilan lowered the plain black, hinged coffin lid.

Thunk.

The lid closed. I felt like a child being put to bed, trapped in a box. I pushed the lid open, then let it close. I didn't hint it to Zhilan, but I also felt safer than any night since becoming a vampire. The total darkness and undeniable sensation of security felt much more appropriate than being under a bed surrounded by blankets and pillows. The fresh reminder that my very instincts had changed upset me a little, but I understood that I belonged in the coffin.

It wasn't because I thought of myself as having died, or being some kind of corpse animated anew with each setting sun. On the contrary, I felt more alive than ever. My heart beat with greater conviction. But as a creature of the night, and considering the source of my newfound vigor, I considered myself part of an underworld separate from humanity. The box, below ground in the basement, made sense.

Zhilan had explained that I could wake up during the day,

if danger approached. I might sense it on my own, but just in case, a high-tech alarm system of sensors and cameras in and around the house would shake the coffin until I opened the lid. Zhilan said that even in a basement with no windows, it would hurt to wake up with the sun shining overhead, but that it would hurt less than what humans might to do me while I slept. She had also told me that I could not read vampires' minds when drinking from them. My experience with Christopher was how it worked for all vampires.

Wearing the same bloodstained clothes, I rested my head on a small pillow and my back on a thin, dark gray, satin-lined mattress. I touched the cushioned walls, only a few inches to my sides. I slid my body down and reached out with my bare feet to the soft end of the coffin. I placed my palms on the underside of the wooden lid. The confinement felt safer, but was still going to take some getting used to.

Blood! Thick blood oozed from Christopher's neck into my mouth.

My eyes opened. Just as I had promised, I had made him pay. Alexander would be next.

I pushed the lid all the way up and climbed out of the coffin. Zhilan, wearing black pants and a red sleeveless top, leaned against the wall near the staircase. Her hair was up, and she wore boots with high heels. As usual, her whole appearance was crisp, right down to her bright red lipstick.

I stretched my neck. Not only did I feel terrible, but I probably looked a mess. "I'm hungry."

I wanted to go to Zhilan's, grab a sword, and get to learning how to use it, but I couldn't focus on that until feeding. Unexpectedly, blurting out about my hunger to Zhilan was therapeutic. She understood my pain.

"We'll go out, then," Zhilan said.

I recalled more details of the previous night's battle. "I need to shower."

"No, you don't." Zhilan smiled. "Aside from the hair on your head, if you are not covered in dirt, you really don't need to bathe anymore. But shower if you want, I will wait."

I went to the bathroom and shut the door. We were in the basement of a house Zhilan was letting me use. She had told me she would send people to deal with everything at Toby's. I had never really had a plan for that, so her help came as a relief.

We were a few blocks south of Pentagon City, a few blocks south of the Pentagon, which sat across the river from D.C. Zhilan lived less than a mile away in a big house overlooking the area. My place had two bedrooms on the second floor, and a living room and kitchen at ground level. It was an old house, with wood floors upstairs, except for linoleum in the kitchen. The basement was more modern, carpeted in light gray with fluorescent lighting. The ceiling was low, and a wooden dresser and standing closet rested against the dark gray walls. All in all, the basement felt pretty cozy.

Zhilan expected me to be safe there, with her so close, as long as I didn't draw unnecessary attention to myself. She made me swear not to hurt any people on my block. She knew most of them and had instructed them to tell her if anything happened. I swore I wouldn't, but Zhilan didn't look completely convinced, so she promised to kill me herself if I did anything to them. My shock must have been evident because she seemed satisfied that would be a sufficient deterrent.

With Zhilan waiting, I decided to skip the shower. I went out and rummaged through my backpack. I found a black skirt and a dark gray top with short sleeves.

"Cheerful," Zhilan said.

I headed back to the bathroom to change. "I need to do some shopping." With the door cracked open, I added, "And I like black and gray."

"That's fine."

Before we headed upstairs, I put on my taller boots. I really did need other options, and with a new home address, I could finally order things online. When I did, they would be paid for using the credit cards of Ms. Adams, a fictitious woman whose name the house was in. Zhilan explained that I should fund Ms. Adams's bank account with my own and pay her credit card bills from there. She showed me how to transfer the money secretly.

The night before, I had transferred all of my money to another bank account Zhilan set up for me in Switzerland. The Swiss had remained neutral with regard to politics between the Sanguans and the Spectavi, and while the Spectavi hadn't yet gone after Sanguan money in America, moving my money seemed prudent.

The floor creaked as we walked across the living room. A

lone lamp sat on an end table beside a black sofa with a coffee table in front of it. A flat-screen TV on a black stand was the only other thing in the room. The walls were bare. While not a priority, I would eventually have to add some art and furniture.

The door locked automatically behind me. Later, what appeared to be no more than a key hole for a deadbolt would scan my thumb. My fingerprint would still work for that, and it definitely beat having to carry a key.

"Do the Spectavi know where you live?" I asked. The moon was nearly full overhead in the clear sky.

"They know, but I would not be an easy target if they came after me. They know that, as well. And if things did go badly, I would not be too proud to flee. Remember that. You will not grow new limbs. If fully drained of blood, you will die, but otherwise, your vampire body can take a great deal. Fire will burn you, but even those marks will fade eventually. Remember that you are fast, and you will heal to live and fight another night."

I nodded. "And the sun's lethal?"

"Yes. You will likely find the weakest light of twilight tolerable, but direct rays from the risen sun will kill you. You may last a few seconds and burn before the end, and if you survive, they say the pain stays with you for quite a while."

We started off, side by side, through the neighborhood. Some houses were a little larger, and others a little smaller, but most were close to the size of mine. Most also appeared similarly old. With that thought, I asked, "How old are you?"

"I wondered if you would ever ask. I became a vampire in 1738."

Being so absorbed with myself, I hadn't expected to be so interested in Zhilan's story, but I really was. "In China?"

"In Italy."

My body ached, and a deep pain in my stomach stopped me in my tracks. I'd have to ask her about Italy later. "I need to feed. I'm sorry."

"That's where we're going."

"Do you have a car? Can we drive? Or run?"

"Yes, I have a car. Yes, I *can* drive. No, we will not be driving, nor will we be running."

I almost hissed at her. "Please? It hurts so much."

She resumed walking. "Tell me what happened at Eure."

Why was she being so cruel? We crossed another block, and I decided where to begin. "A couple of months after I wouldn't leave with you, I found out Edmond was lying… the night Grant was brought in. Wait, have you heard from Grant?"

"Grant is fine. The twins freed most of the Sanguans at Eure, and I met him the following night. Grant asked about you, but I had not found you yet."

Genuine happiness came over me for the first time in days, not the high that came with blood, but real, natural joy. As a human, I had accepted that Grant lusted for me, but trusted him in spite of it. As a vampire, I understood why he'd always made sure to satisfy his hunger before seeing me. I wondered what he would think of me after my transformation, and as someone who hadn't raised a finger while watching him be condemned to death. I hoped he'd forgive me as Zhilan had.

At the end of the block, a row of restaurants and bars were to our left.

"Here?" I asked.

"No, this is on our way. It is too close to home." She headed down the crowded street.

"Let's go up a block. Please?" I didn't think I could handle being among all the people.

"Tell me what else happened at Eure."

I caught up to her in an instant. Once I slowed, I couldn't help watching the men and women walking around us. Some avoided us, while others stared at us. Any one of them would do.

"Erin? After Grant was brought in?" she prompted.

"Um, that night I figured out Edmond was lying. The court and the news stories were a farce. I know you told me some of the Sanguans were innocent. I'm sorry I doubted you."

"It's fine. We have tried to expose that court, but no one listens."

"The next night, while Edmond was reading in his limo, I ran down to where he kept the twins. I thought he had been lying about them, too. I thought they weren't evil. Or at least they might not be. I assumed they knew the truth about Vera, and I didn't really care about anything else." Amidst all the people I craved on the long block, I noticed a few vampires, possibly sizing up prey, and became intensely jealous of them.

"And then?" Zhilan prodded.

I snapped out of it. "And then I cut off the synthetic blood that ran to them, and they woke up. They killed Edmond and confirmed what he had told me—that I had been Vera. As her, I had tried to 'cure' his sisters by altering their synthetic blood, so they attacked me in my dreams. Edmond did what he did to me so I'd leave Eure and have a normal life. That part of his plan didn't exactly work out."

"Edmond was often cruel," Zhilan said. "He always claimed to be a defender of humanity, but over and over, when it served his ends, he made cold, calculating choices that crushed individuals."

We reached the end of the block. "What did he do to you?" I had assumed her hatred for Edmond came solely from his role with the Spectavi.

Zhilan stopped, and I did the same. "He killed my father when I was a young girl."

"Why?"

"I will tell you another time. Let's go down to the subway."

"The subway? You're kidding." I couldn't wait any longer.

"No, we are going to Alexandria."

"Why don't we run? Or take a cab?" It was only a few miles away.

"No."

My insides roared, and I darted past her. I'd feed first and then come back and find her.

Zhilan sped past me. I stopped in front of her.

"If you want me to help you," she said, "if you want me to teach you how to fight, you will listen to me. You did well to make it past all the people back there. As I said, that is too close to home. You may feed in Alexandria."

She walked to the subway escalator, and I followed.

———————

Between the subway station we got out of and the Potomac River, Old Town Alexandria included a mile of bars, restaurants, and shops. Thankfully, Zhilan didn't make me suffer on that particular crowded strip. Instead, we walked parallel, two blocks up the grid of mostly row houses and tall tree after tall tree.

After crossing the main street at its end, we continued for four blocks, until coming to a small, hardly noticeable bar. The night was almost three hours old, and every additional minute was agony.

"Here?" I pleaded.

"Yes."

I turned to the wooden door and grabbed the iron handle.

"Why didn't you kill Heather?" Zhilan surprised me with her question.

"What?" I just wanted to go in and end my pain.

"There must have been a reason. Why did you let her live?"

I remembered vividly. I let go of the handle. "She had two young children. Emily was only a baby. Heather loved her children, and I didn't want them to grow up without their mother."

"Do you think there is someone in there like that?" Zhilan asked.

"A mother of young children? How should I know? How do you know I wouldn't kill them anyway?"

"You could ask them. It does not have to be a mother. You could talk to someone and learn about them instead of attacking."

The lion roared and left a sharp pain when she finished. Maybe another night I'd take my time, when I hadn't been starving for hours. I ran inside.

The bright blue shirt of a man sitting on a bar stool was impossible to miss in the dim room. Scanning around while speeding to him, I didn't notice anyone else. I lifted him, and his mug of beer fell to the ground and shattered.

A wooden staircase wound behind a wall, and I carried the man up. Both doors on the landing at the top were locked. I could have broken them down, but didn't bother trying. I pushed him into the corner and bit his neck.

His blood didn't disappoint. My pain faded almost immediately.

Thump... thump... thump.

The fire burned and flared to a steady drum. I loved every magnificent beat. Why had I let Zhilan make me wait?

Greg was single. He had no family. He was just another accountant.

Thump... thump... thump.

I saw his community college, and then the small university he transferred to. I remembered, as he did, the long hours working job after job to pay his student loans. He had no siblings. He couldn't remember his parents, but he could remember the orphanage where he had been raised.

I stopped, pulled out my fangs, and leaned away from him. Poor little orphan Greg. He opened his eyes. I took two steps back down the stairs.

"Are you all right, Greg?" Zhilan stood at the bottom.

"Yeah," Greg said from behind me. "I'm fine."

"If you would both please join us downstairs." Zhilan walked out of sight.

We descended back into the main room. Two families sat in booths on the wall near the door—parents and two children in one, and a family of five in the other. They all wore dark colors. Greg sat back down at the bar, his shirt collar stained red. I wiped my mouth with the back of my hand. The bartender I hadn't noticed gave him a new beer.

Zhilan stood in the middle of the room. "Erin, these are the Millers, and these are the Reeds. They are your neighbors. Greg is really an orphan, but was asked to be here tonight."

Some of the kids smiled at me. The parents did not.

"I'm sorry… everyone." I rushed outside and down two blocks. How could I have done that in front of all those people, including my new neighbors?

Zhilan caught up to me.

I screamed, "What was I supposed to do? I'm a vampire!"

She remained calm. "Talk to him. Learn his name. Find out he is an orphan *before* you drink from him."

"He would have told me he was an orphan?"

"Yes, he had been instructed to. You also would have found out that he would have welcomed your bite, as long as you did not take his life."

"I was starving!"

"Erin, I assure you, as much pain as you were in, you could have gone the whole night without feeding and then woken up to deal with it tomorrow. You need to be patient."

Patience didn't interest me at all. "Where can I find Alexander? Do you know where Todd is? I don't have time for this!"

"Yes, you do. You have all the time in the world now. So do Alexander and Todd."

I clenched my fists. I ran another block, and Zhilan caught up to me.

"Let's go home," she said. "You could have done worse. Greg is still alive."

We walked all the way back to my house, which Zhilan said was almost five miles. The people we passed interested me, but since I had fed, didn't drive me crazy. Instead, my thoughts drifted between Alexander, Todd, and sword fighting.

Zhilan asked more about my time at Eure. She had never heard of Edmond's brother and had a hunch that very few had. And she had never seen the twins herself. They had been captured before she became a vampire, and efforts to free them—undertaken by others—had been unsuccessful. For a long time, no one knew where they had been hidden, or was even certain they remained alive, until I had set them free.

When I described my escape, William came to mind for the first time since that night.

"With the twins out there, he must have gone back for something extremely important," Zhilan said. "Unfortunately, a silver case is not a lot to go on. It could have been anything."

With no guess to offer, I came up with a question of my own. "Why didn't I know that you knew Greg, when I drank from him?"

"Because I didn't know him. I hired him using a third party. And you were not looking for that information. You were in such a rush, and so unfocused, that stronger memories came to you first, all at once. I assumed, correctly, that you would quickly find his orphan upbringing."

Even as she explained it, I could picture the email chain containing details of his payment, what to wear, and what to tell me if we spoke. Zhilan's name didn't show up in any memory I could find.

"Remember, your neighbors know who you are. They will let me know if you so much as threaten them."

"I won't. I swear." I hated thinking about them after my actions in the bar. Zhilan's threat seemed very real, and if I had my way, I'd never see them again. Eager to change the subject, I asked, "Why don't my ear piercings close up?"

"They remain, like your tattoo, because you chose to get them as a human. New ones would heal."

"I see." I thought of something bigger. "Why didn't you tell me the twins in my dreams were Edmond's sisters?"

"Edmond went to extraordinary lengths to hide his family secret. Those who spread that truth—humans or vampires—were usually dealt with swiftly and mercilessly. It was safer for all of us not to reveal it to you."

I would have liked to have known. But then, Edmond would surely have found out I did, one way or another, and I had no idea how he would have reacted. Dwelling on it was pointless. "How is the… war going?"

"Not well."

That was my impression.

Zhilan continued, "We are about a third less than ten years ago. The Spectavi have gotten very efficient at wiping us out. The court you worked in at Eure is a recent example. Our fighting has become mostly guerilla in nature—small units, ambushes, raids."

"Are there more Spectavi?"

"Yes. There used to be more Sanguans, but with synthetic blood, cooperation increased between the Spectavi and human governments in most of the world. Since then, they have been killing us faster than we reproduce. At this rate, in another ten years, they will cut our numbers in half, and if things don't change, a few decades after that, there will not be many Sanguans left in this country."

I hadn't imagined the situation was quite so dire. "That's awful."

"It will be all right. Before my time, Edmond came close to wiping us out more than once, but we have always found a way to bounce back."

"Why don't we just make more? Can I… make another vampire?"

Zhilan gave me a strained look. "You are not old enough yet. When you are, it is an important decision who to pass on your gifts to. You don't see it yet, but it can be hard to watch the world and its people age, while you do not. Not everyone is truly capable of being an immortal.

"If you do make one, it's a significant emotional investment. You will feel compelled to teach your fledgling how to survive. Some feel it stronger than others, but regardless, other vampires will hold you responsible for the actions of your offspring, especially when those offspring are young. One of the most important considerations is that you cannot do it all the time. Or at least you should not.

"To answer your question, we could each create a new vampire once or twice a year, but we have found that the longer we wait between them, the stronger they will be. Doing it more than once or twice a decade results in offspring who are very frail. This war is no place for a vampire who is not capable of fighting or will not heal when they do. The worst of them are barely stronger than the humans they need to hunt to survive. Those vampires do not last long at all."

"Have you made any?"

"Yes." Zhilan hadn't turned to me to answer.

"How many?"

"A few."

"What happened to them?"

She took a few steps in silence. "I have not heard from one in over a hundred years. Another I do speak to, and see, from time to time. One was killed by the Spectavi." She took another few steps. "Describe again how Edmond died."

I did, and we walked and talked, mile after mile. My vampire body never tired one bit.

It was close to one o'clock by the time we reached the circular drive of Zhilan's large brick house. It had two stories, bright white trim, and was one of the larger homes in the area. The front door opened when we approached, held by a man wearing a white Mandarin shirt and loose black pants.

"Thank you, Tao," Zhilan said as we entered.

Tao closed the door behind us and walked out of sight through a dark room to the left.

Marble covered the floor of the foyer, and a staircase in front of us led up and overlooked it. On the way to a door not far from us, I noticed wood floors and large area rugs in other rooms. Colorful oriental furniture and art stood out in spite of the low lighting. Everything was very neat and clean.

We headed down a staircase, around three corners, before a bright light emanated from below. At the bottom, we stepped into a huge, well lit room, and stood on a rectangular wooden landing. Zhilan took off her shoes, so I sat down on the second to last stair and did the same. I followed her onto a firm foam floor.

The basement was a spacious rectangular gym, which with a few side rooms, had to extend under the whole area of the house above. Racks filled with numerous types of swords and other weapons of varying sizes ran along the tall, wood-paneled wall nearest us. The weapons were stacked two or three high, a little below eye level.

Zhilan walked to the middle of the room, and I followed her until she stopped. She turned and punched me hard in the shoulder.

"Ow!" I yelled, falling to the ground.

She smiled. "Before you touch a weapon, you need to be able to defend yourself and fight without one."

The pain in my shoulder went away quickly. Getting back up, I couldn't help smiling. I still didn't have a sword. But it was the beginning, and I couldn't wait to get started.

By the time I left Zhilan's at around six thirty, almost every part of my body had been beaten and bruised. She was such a delicate-looking little creature, but her repeated blows drove home the point that appearances meant nothing. Her lightning speed and tremendous strength made me wonder more about her, but I had decided against interrupting her instruction to ask about Italy.

We had gone over footwork, blocking, and basic punching and kicking. Zhilan explained that as a vampire, I should learn quickly. If I focused, I should be good at mimicking what she did. She was right, and I guessed there was something else at work that I didn't mention. I had an inkling that as Vera, I may have already known some of what Zhilan taught me. In a few short hours with Zhilan, I became significantly more competent.

I limped back to my basement alone, and changed into boxers and a t-shirt. I inspected the deep gash under my left eye. Almost immediately, it had stopped bleeding, but it hadn't gone away. According to Zhilan, the cut would heal. She had said the same thing about the deep, purple bruise on my left thigh and the sharp pain in my right knee.

A few aching steps brought me near my coffin, and I surveyed the room. My laptop sat on a simple white desk. A black mesh office chair was in front of it. I was surrounded by empty drawers and empty closets. I could picture the complete set of furniture on glossy pages of a catalogue.

For the third time I could remember, I found myself alone somewhere completely foreign. Fear and a familiar nausea crept into my mind and body. I succeeded in pushing them away. Being scared had gotten me nowhere in the past. I would be stronger. My tongue ran from fang to fang. There was no excuse not to be stronger.

I climbed into my coffin, rested my head on the small pillow, and lowered the lid.

7

The lion held a bleeding deer carcass in her mouth. The deer faded, body first, then antlers, until it had disappeared completely.

I stared up at the lid and carefully pushed it open. No one appeared to be around, as expected. I climbed out of my coffin and plopped down at my desk. My laptop said five after seven. Zhilan was coming at seven thirty.

My knee didn't hurt anymore, and my thigh was no longer bruised. My fingertips searched for the gash under my eye but couldn't find it. Strolling with Zhilan the night before, after feeding, I had occasionally felt so human. Considering my healed injuries, and as the pit in my stomach grew, I did not.

I didn't have a lot of time, but I noticed an email from the *Shattered Nights Newsletter*, reminding me of the band's show the next day. I put on their music while getting dressed and made a mental note to buy external speakers for my laptop as soon as possible.

With a few minutes before Zhilan would arrive, I googled Alexander. Going down the list of familiar results, I opened web pages I had already visited and found nothing new: sketches of a big Greek vampire believed to be over five hundred years old, a few blurry pictures, rumors of crimes he was responsible for and a long list of possible locations of his primary whereabouts. When the last link opened, what I saw shocked me. A sharp photo posted three days earlier showed what appeared to be the same vampire up close. He had only one arm—his right was missing—and both of his feet were crude metal prosthetics, according to the caption.

I compared the new image to the old ones, and it seemed possible they were of the same Sanguan. Disfigured vampires were rare, and Alexander had more than just a few scars.

———————

Zhilan's two-door black Mercedes was the nicest non-limousine car I had ever been in. The interior was soft beige leather and wooden trim. Her aggressive driving matched the sporty body. Best of all, she didn't make me walk the ten miles to the bar she had in mind.

Cain had a reputation as a meeting place for vampires and willing humans. With little doubt about finding someone to drink from, the real question was if I could pick someone I wouldn't kill when feeding. Zhilan had insisted I try my best to make that happen.

The identity of the night's impending meal didn't matter to me. Whether I tried to or not, I kept picturing the lion and the disappearing carcass. The hungry cat wanted her meal back.

But I did worry about what Zhilan would do if I killed

someone. While she preached patience, I felt I was only a few steps away from getting a shot at Alexander. On top of the training, she had to know where to find him, so my quest for revenge would probably be a lot more difficult without her.

As the bar door opened, the rock music and additional light were welcome changes from all the clubs in the city. A few people and vampires noticed us when we walked in, but I had expected even more attention. Zhilan looked pretty great in her short black skirt and purple top. My light gray skirt was longer, and my pale blue shirt not quite as fancy. When Zhilan had seen my black pumps, she had a predictable line ready about me owning something other than boots.

More usefully, she had given me a small black pouch attached to a band that strapped around my thigh like the one I had seen her use when paying at the subway the night before. It was a modified gun holster for the outside of my leg, and she had explained that she had grown tired of dealing with a purse when things got unexpectedly hectic. That made sense to me. The pouch wasn't easily noticeable under my skirt, and it was pretty cool.

We sat down at the wooden bar on simple wooden stools. Anyone would have done: one of the Goths sitting near us, one of the Goths at the booths lining the walls, one of few non-Goths who seemed so out of place. Guy or girl, I wouldn't be picky.

"Zhilan." A vampire in a long black jacket and dark slacks walked up behind us. He was bald, wore a navy button-down shirt, and his ebony skin had hardly lightened, so he couldn't have been especially old.

I followed her lead when Zhilan turned around on her stool. "Ben, hello," she said.

"I didn't expect to see *you* here," Ben responded.

Zhilan tilted her head my way. "This is Erin. She's new."

Ben bowed his head. "Nice to meet you."

"Nice to meet you." As at Night, a satisfying feeling came over me. While I knew nothing about the Sanguan, he didn't scare me at all. I belonged in his vampire world and was one of the hunters at the bar, just like him.

"Erin, you look famished. I could recommend someone if you'd like." Ben motioned toward the crowd, then looked past me and smiled at someone halfway down the bar.

The offer tempted me for a moment, but ultimately, it seemed too weird. "Thank you, but no. I'll be fine."

"Suit yourself." Ben put his hands together up near his chest. "Zhilan, Erin, have a good night, and I hope to see you both soon." He headed past the bar to the rear of the building.

"Who's he?" I asked.

"A friend. He works with us sometimes," Zhilan answered, presumably meaning with Grant, and, before he was killed, James. We turned back to the bar. "Are you not hungry?"

"Huh?"

"I thought you were starving. Aren't you going to go talk to anyone?"

In my mind, I played out slamming someone against the wall, blocking out their memories, and being done with them. I wanted to feel better and get back to Zhilan's basement. I wanted a sword.

I tried to give Zhilan a scowl, but my expression ended up closer to a plea. She didn't react. With a deep breath, I got up and walked to the other side of the bar to a boy I had noticed earlier.

When I took the stool to his right, he stopped talking to his friend on the other side. I smiled when he turned to me. The boy's long black bangs covered much of his white painted face. He wore all black, and in spite of my intense craving for his blood, I really did wonder what his story was.

"I'm Erin."

"Tim," he responded. "Do you want some blood?"

Tim had gotten straight to the point. "Um, maybe. What do you do, Tim?"

"Nothing." He was apparently not a big talker.

"Nothing?"

"Nothing that matters. I work in the mall. I sell TVs and stereos. I come here at night." He wasn't as mysterious as I had hoped. "You can have some blood if you want it." He rolled up his sleeve and presented his wrist. A fresh bite mark shown prominently against the faded scars of old ones.

I stood up. "I don't think that's a good idea." I was confident I'd kill him. "I'm sorry," I added awkwardly, unsure if I should have bothered. I walked back to Zhilan.

"No?" she asked.

"Tim was not so interesting. I didn't think I'd find a reason to let him live." I sat back down. "And I'm not sure he would have minded."

She nodded.

"What about Greg?" I asked. My lips and throat had become parched since leaving Tim. "Could we find him?"

Zhilan considered it for a moment. "Not tonight. You will find it easier to build relationships with people than to find new ones each time, but no Greg tonight."

Ugh. So I had the right idea, but would have to starve a little longer regardless. I crossed my arms on the bar and slumped my head down onto them, looking away from Zhilan. Almost immediately, I picked up my head and turned back. "Aren't you hungry?"

"Not really. I won't feed tonight."

"How often do you?"

"Once a week. Maybe more, maybe less."

"Doesn't it drive you crazy to wait that long?"

"No. One day, it will be so with you."

I turned from her and dropped my head back onto my arms on the bar. I scanned the portion of the room I could see for someone more interesting than Tim. Everything was sideways. How should I know who to go after? What a waste of time.

A keyboard played in the middle of the song coming from the sound system. I closed my eyes and pictured Luke belting vocals to a raucous crowd. He slammed on his piano as *Ember* picked up pace. What if Luke showed up? I imagined racing to him before he got a step past the doorway. No one else could have him.

The stool to my right scraped against the floor, and my eyes shot open. A large man in faded jeans and a tucked-in blue polo shirt sat down. He leaned forward to get the bartender's attention, and the man's gut eclipsed my view. I sat up. The blue of his shirt was too close to the color of his jeans. I got the impression he didn't go to that bar very often.

The bartender brought him a beer. The man sipped it, then noticed me staring at him. "Hi there."

"Hi," I responded. He had a big tan face, and very short, light brown hair.

"I'm Nick."

"I'm Erin." I focused on his stocky neck. "Do you come here often?" Clichéd, but important.

"Nope." Nick took a big swig of his beer. "It's my first time. I heard some things and came to see what this place was all about." He drank some more.

I managed to stop staring at his neck. "What do you do?"

"I'm a mechanic."

That didn't sound like it would work.

He must have noticed my disappointment. "It's all I could find since I've been back home. I fought in Afghanistan."

I perked up. A soldier might do the trick. "Are you married?"

"No."

My own heart picked up speed as I heard his do the same. "Do you have any kids?"

"No. Does it matter?"

I ignored his question. "You know what I am?"

Nick had another drink, then answered to his glass. "Yes."

I turned to Zhilan, who calmly said, "Here is fine, or in the back room, or outside around back."

I turned back to Nick. "Do you want to go outside?"

"Sure." The big man swallowed the last of his beer and got up. He took two steps toward the door before suddenly remembering manners that didn't concern me at that moment. "After you."

I led, and from behind me, he muttered, "That didn't take long."

Under the overcast sky, the brick side of the bar we walked around was very dark. Nick wasn't wearing a coat, so it probably wasn't that cold. A thin concrete path ran between the wall and dark brown mulch and plants.

I hadn't been nervous with any of the others, but the buildup to that… test was different. We reached the back of the building, and under a floodlight, two vampires—one man and one woman—were feeding on people.

We stopped, and I couldn't help picturing myself as a weak girl at the mercy of one of those creatures. I hated the thought. Nick appeared terrified. I grabbed his arm and walked us back a few steps to the darker side wall so the others were out of sight.

He opened his mouth to say something, but my fangs pierced his neck before he got a word out.

Heat.

I wrapped my arm around Nick's back and brought the big man close. Nick's body felt so good to hold. I sucked harder. The fire burned higher, and my hunger whimpered away.

Nick had always excelled in training. He pushed himself to be the best soldier he could be.

My insides became blue hot, as the good man's blood fueled the flames.

He had been brave in Afghanistan. Men rallied around him when they were ambushed.

Oh, my God. The lion kept feasting.

When the grenade went off, Nick watched as two in his unit were blown apart. He had known them for years and remembered with horrible detail the terror in their faces the instant before it happened. Another grenade flew through the air.

I pulled my teeth out of him. Tears slid down my cheeks while my chest heaved.

"That was…" He brought his arm up between us and wiped sweat off his forehead. "… incredible. Are you an angel?"

I let him go. "What?"

The soldier glanced down at my neck, at my cross.

"No," I said. "Not even close."

He turned to watch me leave, and stuck his arm out against the wall for support. "Thank you," he called.

Zhilan stood near the entrance, scrolling through something on her phone.

I headed straight for her car. "Let's go."

———————

My tears had dried before we got to her car, but I didn't speak until nearly back at Zhilan's place. "How did you deal with it?"

"Deal with what?"

"When you were young. How did you deal with the hunger, the killing, the awful things you saw when you drank every night."

Zhilan kept her eyes on the road. "Not as well as you."

"He was supposed to have been too good a person for me to bring myself to kill, with no wife and kids in case I failed. But he had seen such terrible things in war. Now I can see them." As the visions raced through my mind, remembering Toby, and then honey-filled Ashley, gave me some peace. "I didn't feel this way after the first few."

She turned to me briefly. "But this one is alive. Did he enjoy it?"

"Yes."

"Think about what you have given him for a moment. Think about how it compares to the war he fought in. He came to the bar for exactly the rush of euphoria that you gave him, while you got what you craved."

I didn't say anything, so Zhilan kept going. "Would you rather not have seen his memories, and have killed him?"

At the moment, yes. I wasn't sure if my conscious had really survived my second rebirth as Zhilan hoped. Maybe it had; I hadn't been able to kill Heather after learning of her children. But the idea of having killed her if I hadn't known didn't seem to bother me. And why shouldn't I use my ability to shield myself from disturbing memories like Nick's? The visions had been so awful, and would be hard, if not impossible, to forget.

Zhilan spoke of the value of Nick's life, but what about

mine? After all I had been through, why should I deal with limitations and compromises? It should by *my* time, finally, to get *my* way. As a vampire, that meant having *who* I wanted.

But I chose not to have that debate with her. Needing her to think I was coming along, I said, "I guess it was better this way."

———————————

Zhilan, wearing red pants and a robe tied at the waist and fit for fighting, waited near the wall in her basement. I emerged from a room near the staircase in a black version of the same outfit. Seeing where she was, I rushed to her. Mounted horizontally on the wall in front of us were two identical straight swords with short handles.

"Calm down," she said. "Take one, and do nothing but hold it."

I eagerly grabbed the one on top. Zhilan stepped back and watched me. The shiny blade was just over an inch wide and a little longer than two feet. With my right hand up against the brown guard that separated the blade and the handle, I squeezed my left hand on to the little space remaining below it. Holding the sword with one hand didn't feel comfortable, nor did having two on the handle.

"Have you ever held a sword before?" Zhilan asked.

"Uh, probably. After she beat me to a pulp, Victoria mentioned something about training Vera. So technically, she trained *me*."

"Did she?"

I nodded, failing to mention how good she said I had been.

Zhilan took the sword away from me and put it back on the wall. "Try one of these." She pointed at the two swords to the right of the first. The blades were of similar width, but a little longer and with a slight curve. The handles were significantly longer.

I grabbed the top sword near the guard with my right hand, and immediately brought my left to the bottom of the handle, leaving a few inches between my hands. That felt good.

"That is a Japanese katana. Victoria uses one sometimes. It appears you have held one before." Zhilan took the sword from me and gripped it as I had. She turned to the side, raised the blade over her head, stepped forward, and cut down. "I can teach you to fight with it again."

My wooden bokken cut through the air, exactly as Zhilan had shown me with hers. She feared I would injure myself with a steel blade, and if the wound was bad, it could be permanent, so we stuck with the wooden bokken.

We spent a few hours working on footwork, positions, and then me cutting into thin air. A little of the previous night's instruction applied, while the rest was new—except not. After she told me something once, nothing *really* seemed new.

I brought my bokken above my head and started to cut down. My elbows were out wider than they should have been.

"Bring your elbows in toward each other," Zhilan said. "Do it again. Your elbows must be tighter."

I raised my bokken and did it again, correctly.

"Good," Zhilan said.

It was as though I had done it a million times. When I did things correctly, it felt correct. When I made mistakes, I usually sensed having done so before Zhilan told me. I often guessed exactly how to fix them.

We started to spar, and unlocking my hidden talent became breathtaking at every turn. Zhilan had to have seen it on my face because she responded with her own, more subtle excitement. She had been serious and stern almost continuously since the night on the roof, but finally let her guard down a bit, in the face of my eagerness.

Her instruction was giving me part of my old life back. As Vera, I had to have spent years learning the techniques, and in Zhilan's basement, we discovered that Edmond hadn't driven them from me permanently. I relished that small failure of his.

Thwack!

Zhilan smacked me in the side with her bokken. "Good," she said. "But your swings are too long. They are a waste of time. Your sword will be sharp, and you will almost always be able to generate enough power without a long swing. That's true of any vampire, and certainly of you. Stick to short, compact cuts."

I did as she said. We fought for hours.

8

"I am not so sure it's a good idea," Zhilan said over the phone the next night. "I thought we would head back to Cain's tonight, first."

"I'm sorry, but they're playing earlier than scheduled, and I really want to go. I'll be back by ten or eleven," I said.

"Why is this so important?"

Luke. *Ember.* Going to Cain's again didn't excite me, but the real answer was Luke. "I… I've liked these guys for a while, and I haven't had a chance to see them recently."

"Be careful, Erin. Feed before you go."

"Okay. Bye." I hung up.

Shattered Nights had played on my laptop as I fell asleep, and while listening to them after climbing out of my coffin, an email showed up, letting me know that they were playing two hours earlier than scheduled. Instead of having to choose between Zhilan and seeing their show, I would be able to do both.

My body ached to be fed, but it was after seven o'clock, and I didn't have time to find someone and get to know them before eight. I told myself that I could make it until the band finished, then feed, and get back to training.

I chose one of my shorter skirts, then put on lots of dark eye shadow for the first time as a vampire. With my slightly lighter skin, and especially once I made my lips paler to match, my eyes stood out even more than normal. It was a long shot, but on the off chance Luke glanced my way in the crowd, he might notice them.

The old building off V Street in Northwest, D.C. was essentially a big industrial room with small bars on both sides. It wasn't as dark as I expected, perhaps because it was so early and another band would come on later. I arrived a few minutes after eight o'clock to the steady drumbeats of what I hoped was Shattered Nights's first song. I recognized it as one of my downloads.

The crowd was still small, but when Luke began singing, everyone present came to attention and bobbed their heads to the song. I made my way to the far left of the room, in front of the bar and behind the crowd, and watched intently.

Luke looked so much better in person than in the online videos. A subtle shine came off his black pants. His white shirt had tight sleeves and a low neck. I was so glad to have come.

By the end of the song, people's entire bodies were into it. The last drumbeat hit, and in the brief calm that followed, my hunger screamed to be dealt with. I leaned against the wall and tried to focus on the music as it resumed. I failed, and began sizing up the other band members.

Gwen, the bassist, was tall and skinny. She wore a black dress over red tights and had very dark brown hair that covered most of her face. I wondered exactly when she and Luke had been a couple. Joe, the lead guitar player, wore jeans and a blue shirt. He had brown hair, an average build, and his thing was being the most clean-cut member of the group. He wasn't bad looking. Jonathan played the drums. He was the shortest, and his black hair was a mess.

From what I had found, they all had their fans, but Luke had the most by far.

The next few songs were minute after minute of me struggling to ignore those who came near me. The hunk with dark olive skin had to be delicious. I traced the toned muscles in his lower back under his black shirt—or just imagined I could make them out. A girl in a tight red dress stole my attention, as she was stealing it from so many others. If I had worn that dress, I wouldn't have to bother hunting. Men would be flocking to me. An aspect of my power that I hadn't considered yet came to mind: tasting the woman in red, I could taste what she experienced when they flocked to her.

Luke sat down at the piano. Thank goodness. I should have fed before the show.

The crowd had filled in considerably and grew quiet. Luke hit the first keys.

He walked away…

She cried away.

I loved that song so much. It started slower than all their others, and Luke sang alone for all of it. Transfixed with every part of him, I only caught portions of his lyrics.

She moved away.

My head hurt because I was so thirsty. I stood up straight off the wall.

Over Gwen's steady beats from the bass, Luke hit a high note, but he did it softly so it wasn't startling. His voice came back down, while the piano remained at the high end. I loved the range in his singing. He picked up speed, and the crowd bobbed with him.

His hope still burns.

They bobbed faster and faster, and most of the crowd sang along.

I couldn't join in either activity. I had to focus completely on Luke. The emotion in his face built and built as the song went on—sorrow when the man left his girlfriend, hope when he decided he wanted her back, pain when she moved away and he couldn't find her, joy when she found him.

Luke finished softly.

Their love still burns.

The crowd went wild.

Luke stepped back up to the standing microphone. "Thank you, guys." He surveyed the crowd. "Thank you!" His captivating brown eyes came my way. I had to have him. The lion let loose a thunderous roar. I would race to Luke and taste him in a matter of seconds. Less.

"These guys rock." The voice came from a short man to my right. When I glanced back at the stage, Luke was getting ready for the next song.

I turned again to the short man. "Yeah." He had dark hair and was good looking. I pictured myself at his neck. I could have Luke after him. Why not do it? But I didn't know anything about him. The lion roared again. No one would notice. So what if he died? I looked at Luke, then back at the man who was close enough to bite.

I sped outside, bumping into a few people on the way.

I raced south for Virginia as quickly as possible, to regain my composure there. Turning the corner after four blocks, I knocked into a woman, who dropped her groceries. When I recognized the two boxes of children's cereal that hit the asphalt, I pulled her into an alley and held the diamond of her solitaire ring tightly between my fingers while drinking from her fragile neck. I left Nicole slumped against the wall, still breathing.

At the sound of police sirens, I darted to the end of the block, then zigzagged for a few more blocks before heading south.

My phone rang while I was taking off my makeup back home. Physically, I felt incredible once more, but Nicole hadn't been what I truly craved. While I had succeeded in letting her live, she wasn't Luke, or any of the other men from the show. She wasn't the woman in the red dress I had envied. Nicole wasn't exciting at all.

"Hi, Zhilan," I said.

"Erin, I have to help with a job right away. You should come."

"Okay."

"I will be by in ten minutes. Wear black. I know you have plenty." She hung up.

I changed into black athletic pants and a black long-sleeved shirt with a high, rounded neck. Black flat shoes seemed like my best option. Fighting Christopher in heels hadn't been a problem; my balance as a vampire seemed perfect. But those boots weren't quiet, and the shoes were.

I put my hair up and went outside to wait, wondering what we could be doing and excited for whatever it would end up being. Nicole and the sirens faded from my mind.

Zhilan's car came around the corner with Tao driving. She had told me he helped keep her home and affairs in order, and when I asked if she drank from him, she said nothing beyond a simple, "Sometimes." I guessed him to be around thirty years old.

I joined Zhilan in the back seat. She had dressed like me and, while her face appeared perfect, her makeup was more muted than usual. She held her straight sword in its scabbard on her lap.

"Did you bring one for me?" I asked.

"Not tonight. You don't need a sword to watch and learn."

It was a deflating, but not particularly shocking thing for her to say.

———————

Tao drove more sensibly than Zhilan and dropped us off within running distance of our destination near the Beltway.

We were a few miles outside D.C. to hijack a truckload of Spectavi weapons—guns mostly—headed for the city. If successful, we would drive them down to Richmond, Virginia, where Zhilan said some Sanguans were organized.

Zhilan strapped her sword across her back, and I followed her through the woods to a rendezvous point near the highway exit ramp where we would hit the truck. Zhilan instructed me on how to stay quiet as we went. While I couldn't help being nervous, there was also no shortage of excitement. I had never done anything like what we had planned, and I *really* wished I had a sword of my own.

We came to a huge tree in the woods, and a bright light blinded me. A short vampire lowered his flashlight. Grant stood next to him.

"Max, this is Erin. She's watching tonight," Zhilan said.

"Hello, Erin," Max said. Between his black pants and matching vest, he had pockets everywhere. I noticed a handgun at his side, in addition to the assault rifle slung over his shoulder.

"Erin," Grant said, before I could respond to Max. Grant's black turtleneck was a different look for him, but his dark blue jeans came as no surprise. They were also the only non-black attire among all of us. Dark stubble covered part of the big vampire's face, as it often had. I was relieved to see him again, and to see him apparently perfectly healthy. He looked just like the fighter he had before, in spite of how he claimed to have changed over thirty-three years as a vampire.

"I'm sorry, Grant," I said. "I'm sorry I didn't believe you at Eure."

"Don't worry about it. Things must have been hard for you there, and I'm fine, which Zhilan tells me was your doing. Thank you."

I flashed a fake smile. I didn't deserve his thanks.

"Okay," Max broke back into the conversation. "They have a jeep in front of the truck and one in back. I'll be sure the light is red when they get off the highway. Zhilan will take care of the first jeep and the truck driver. Grant will take care of the one in the back, and then he and I will head for the truck. Any questions?" No one said anything. "We've done this before. It should be quick and easy."

Zhilan turned to me. "Erin, go with Grant. When he breaks for the truck, stay where you are. When this is over, I will come find you."

I nodded. Zhilan and Max sped out of sight. Grant inspected the rifle that hung on a strap over his shoulder.

"No sword for you?" I asked.

He gave me a quick grin. "I'll learn one of these days."

I was so thankful my stupidity hadn't cost Grant his life. "I really am sorry."

"It's over. I made it." When he finished brushing aside my apology, he looked concerned. "How are you handling things?"

"Fine, I guess. It's a lot to deal with. My mind's kind of all over the place sometimes." It was a relief to say to someone other than Zhilan.

"You'll be all right. It's only been a few weeks. You've got a lot to learn, but you'll learn it." He checked his watch. "Come on."

He started away between the trees slowly, then picked up speed when it became apparent I could keep up. Before long, the highway and exit ramp came into view. Grant crouched behind another large tree, and I got close to him to stay hidden. A tall streetlight illuminated the intersection in front of us.

Grant whispered, "She wouldn't let you bring any weapon at all?"

"No." It was so frustrating. Surely, I could play *some* helpful role.

He turned back to the road. "If there's ever anything you need to ask, but don't want to ask Zhilan, give me a call."

I remembered how he had wanted to bite my neck and my breasts back at Fire and Ice. He had terrified me, but things had changed. Whatever he thought of me, I had become strong and could stand up for myself. Plus, Zhilan trusted Grant, and so did Max. James had before he died. "Thanks," I whispered back.

A few seconds later, he bolted away from our tree. I quietly moved to where he had been and watched him stop near the edge of the woods. Headlights came down the exit ramp, and then a semi-truck with a blue cab and long white trailer followed. I noticed another large tree ahead, so I darted for it to get a better view.

The leading silver jeep came to rest at the red street light. The truck that followed it did the same. Once the jeep at the rear stopped, all three vehicles idled, bunched together.

Grant raced from the woods, then Zhilan. They each slapped at their target jeep and left something dark attached to the sides of them. A second later, Zhilan hid halfway around the truck trailer, and Grant moved far past the rear vehicle.

As some of the Spectavi leapt clear—*Boom! Boom!*—explosions rocked the jeeps. Those who hadn't fled burned among the broken, twisted metal.

The big truck rammed into what remained of the front jeep to create space to drive around it. The truck reversed, then slammed into the jeep again, and Zhilan leapt at the driver-side door of the blue cab. She held on to the handle while thrusting her jet-black blade through the window. The truck inched forward, and shattered glass fell to the pavement. Gunshots from the Spectavi who had fled the front jeep came at Zhilan. She swung her body backward, then forward again and thrust her sword far into the cab. The truck stopped.

Kicking out with both legs, Zhilan launched herself away from the truck and sped between the three Spectavi shooting at her, slicing one of them along the way. At the rear jeep, Grant moved constantly and returned fire sporadically.

All the Spectavi kept firing, but the two Sanguans moved too quickly and unpredictably for their assailants to get a good fix on them. Zhilan managed to take out another of the Spectavi.

With Spectavi attention away from the big truck, Max emerged from the woods, charging straight for it. When he reached the cab and got in, he opened up on the Spectavi out on the road with his rifle. Grant seized the opportunity to join Max in the truck. He took the wheel and plowed the jeep out of the way.

I allowed myself to relax as the big truck turned to the left, ready to leave the battle behind.

Whoosh-whoosh-whoosh-whoosh came from overhead. A dark green helicopter flew over me, big guns firing. The truck's front windshield shattered, and Max and Grant fled out of it. Zhilan headed for cover at the back of the truck trailer, and then so did they. Max got hit, and then Grant did, and they both slowed. They all made it behind the white trailer.

Five Spectavi jumped down from the helicopter and headed to the rear of the truck. Two drew swords, and instead of waiting for them, Zhilan emerged and attacked. The other three Spectavi fired on Grant and Max.

The Sanguans couldn't have expected the backup from the chopper, or they would have brought more than three for their attack. I ached to be out there with them. With any weapon—a sword, gun, or even a knife—I would have gone. Zhilan had rendered me so helpless. I clenched my hands into fists, hating every second of my useless spectating.

While Zhilan fought, Grant and Max emerged from behind the trailer with their hands behind their heads, surrounded by Spectavi. The two Sanguans knelt on the ground, both bleeding, mostly from their midsections. The helicopter continued to hover low.

A few people had stopped their cars on the highway. A silver SUV raced off the exit ramp and screeched to a halt. Another three Spectavi streamed out, making six with their guns trained on Grant and Max.

After Zhilan sliced the arm off one of her two opponents,

one of the Spectavi guarding Grant and Max put down his rifle and drew a sword to join the attack on her. Zhilan danced between the two of them. She was incredible with that sword—a Chinese *jian*, she had told me—but I didn't know how long she could last. Could she really defeat them both, and all the rest, and then save Grant and Max? Or would she retreat to fight another day? It would be terrible to leave them behind, but maybe also logical.

Pshw! BOOOOM!

The helicopter crashed and exploded not far from the big truck. Everyone turned to the blaze. From the woods just past it, two streaks of black shot out, and three of the Spectavi near Grant were sliced in half at the waist. The other two turned to shoot.

Caterine and Ariane sped over and cut their blades through both of the Spectavi with ease. The twin demons with almost pure white skin stopped and stood in front of the raging fire. They held shiny katanas in their right hands, down at their sides. The white sheets from Edmond's basement had been replaced by black leather pants and sleeveless black tops with red trim. A bullet hole closed on Caterine's shoulder. Her hair was still longer than her sister's.

BOOM!

An explosion came from the downed helicopter. Standing in front of the blaze, the sisters had found a way to look even more terrible than they had at Eure. They sped toward Zhilan and engaged the two Spectavi fighting her. It was so strange to see Zhilan alongside the most ancient Sanguans.

The SUV drove off. Grant and Max got to the truck, and the sword fighting was the lone battle that raged on.

Ariane cut down a Spectavi, who slumped to the ground. A silver arrow hit her thigh.

"Ghaa!" She snapped off the arrow. "Victoria! Show yourself!"

Victoria obliged. Wearing a loose black leather skirt and matching top, the huge warrior flew out of the woods. While only about half as old as the twins, her skin was nearly as white. When she reached the one who had invited her out, she swung her two-handed longsword with purpose, while her tight braid of long black hair whipped around her.

Ariane's smaller blade repelled her, but she seemed hurt from the arrow and struggled as Victoria continued to reign down mighty blow after mighty blow.

A vampire I had never seen shot out of the forest. He was Japanese, dressed in black, and almost as pale as Victoria. When his katana met Ariane's, I knew him to be another Spectavi.

Caterine rushed to help her sister, which left Zhilan alone to deal with the last Spectavi from the helicopter.

A lot less disappointed, I considered myself privileged to witness the dance of those ancient combatants. The Spectavi I didn't know was average height, while the three females were taller. Everyone had a similar length reach of their arms, but Victoria's sword was the longest. Even though time must have rendered her white skin rock solid, Caterine appeared to dart effortlessly from place to place, faster than even Victoria. Victoria and the other Spectavi looked physically stronger, but I had no idea if they really were.

Zhilan sliced off the head of the Spectavi who had kept her occupied for so long, then entered the battle, and the old Spectavi had another opponent. The three Sanguans immediately began to close in on their foes. I couldn't imagine Victoria falling, but that suddenly seemed possible.

The Japanese vampire blocked a blow from Zhilan, moved close, and threw her over his shoulder. Ariane slashed open Victoria's side. Victoria's sword ripped through the outer half of Caterine's arm.

The freshly wounded vampires both jumped backward. Zhilan sprang to her feet and stood ready to rejoin the fight. I never imagined seeing Victoria hurt in battle, but red ran down from under her top. Caterine's wound closed, and a few seconds later, the blood coming from Victoria slowed. The broken arrow remained embedded in Ariane's thigh.

The sisters glanced at each other, sheathed their katanas behind their backs, then ran and jumped up to the highway. They raced off together across the traffic.

Victoria put her big sword on her back. Zhilan did the same with her *jian*. Victoria glanced at the other Spectavi and took a long breath. She looked weary. The two Spectavi sped off after the twins.

———————

Before sunrise that morning, I lay on my back in my coffin with the lid open and Shattered Nights playing on a loop from my laptop. I couldn't stop thinking about the battle. The twins were incredible with their katanas, and I yearned to be that good. I couldn't have fought them or Victoria, but I would have liked to have tested myself against the other Spectavi.

That Zhilan had stood alongside the evil sisters continued to fascinate me. It made sense; Victoria had bested Zhilan at Eure. And we *were* all Sanguans. But they were Caterine and Ariane. In Edmond's basement, they seemed an embodiment of pure evil, and it certainly didn't appear that they had calmed down since then.

Ember came on, and I rolled onto my side and recalled Luke's show. He had looked amazing, and I loved the way he controlled the crowd. If I hadn't been so overwhelmed by my hunger, I might have danced a little along with everyone else.

I grabbed the edge of my coffin lid and brought it down. With Luke's voice filling the basement, I closed my eyes and again replayed the battle.

9

Grant and Max had to stop and feed to help them recover, but otherwise made it to Richmond without further incident. The next night, I fed off a young man two weeks away from getting married. He could hardly wait for the day to come, which had been enough for me to let him live. He had been so scared when I left him, thinking I might finish the job. He didn't know how much I would have hated another bite. His thoughts made me sad and worried about Todd. Marriage wasn't in the cards for us any longer, but who knew what our future could hold? If nothing else, I *owed* it to him to rescue him. If I couldn't go after Alexander yet, maybe I should start with Todd.

Crack!

Zhilan's wooden sword collided with mine in her basement. "What's the rush?" Zhilan asked.

"Todd's a victim of Edmond, just like I was. He needs my help."

Crack!

"How do you intend to help him?"

"I'll find him, bring him back here, and figure out what they did to him."

"Please do not bring any Spectavi back here."

"Then I'll bring him to my house." I stepped forward and cut at her.

Crack! Crack!

She stopped again. "What if you are wrong and he left you on his own? Or what if he's too well protected for you to get to?"

"I'm not wrong." I shook my head. "I spent too long thinking the Spectavi could be trusted. And if you come with me, we won't fail." I swung.

Crack! Crack! Crack!

"I would help you. In a few months, when you are ready for something like that."

"A few months! I can't wait that long."

"Yes, you can. You could wait a month, or a year, or ten years." Zhilan came at me.

Crack! Crack! Thwak! Her sword smacked into my thigh.

"Ow!" I ended up ten feet to the left.

Zhilan stood relaxed. "You're learning fast, faster than anyone I have ever instructed. Victoria obviously taught Vera well. But Erin has a lot to learn, including this: it is dangerous to fight when you are distracted. You've been blocking that move all night, but you missed it this time because you are thinking about Todd, having to wait months to go after him, and likely your choices in trusting the Spectavi. It's too much. Find what motivation you will in those things, but when in battle, you cannot get lost in their details. Your focus must be on the fight."

Alexander was also on my mind, but I didn't think

Zhilan would be receptive to any questions concerning him. "What do you think of Caterine and Ariane?"

"Evil," she said quickly. "They are evil."

That did have to be the single best word to describe them. "But we're on the same side of this war. What do you think they'll do?"

"I don't know. The world is so different compared to when they were locked away." Zhilan tapped her bokken against her leg a few times. "They surely want revenge against the Spectavi, against Victoria certainly. She played a significant role in their capture. In that way, they should help our cause. Beyond that, it depends on what exactly they do."

We got back to sparring. It unnerved me that Zhilan was so unsure about Caterine and Ariane, but eventually my focus returned to training. With it, came the extreme satisfaction of regaining stolen skills. I learned a lot as the hours flew by.

While walking home, my newly cut and bruised body made it obvious I was no master with a blade. But I was no novice either. I could already be helpful fighting alongside Zhilan, and if she came with me, we would surely be able to rescue Todd. If nothing else, I had definitely learned enough to have my own sword.

———————

When I woke up the next evening, my laptop speakers got a break from Shattered Nights. A cell-phone-shot video of the battle from two nights prior played full screen. It was dark, low quality, and a little choppy because of how fast all the vampires moved, but having been there, I had no trouble following the action from the new angle.

I watched the twins jump from the ground, off trees, and then up to the low-flying helicopter. They killed the pilot and other Spectavi inside, then leapt away before it crashed to the ground. The swordfight between the ancients was more impressive in my head than in the grainy video, but I watched it twice anyway. The tall females must have been downright gigantic compared to their human contemporaries.

I started to ache for blood. My lips were chapped, and my head hurt. My pain plunged deeper as I considered the prospect of tracking down another parent, engaged person, or someone whose past was so terrible that it brought tears to my eyes when I drank.

A link from the video led to a mess of a website with an article about the battle. Someone else had posted high-quality photos. Ten pictures focused on the twins, and at the bottom of the page, every single comment mentioned them. Men and women alike longed to feel their bites, claiming they didn't care about the consequences. A few people offered wild guesses at their history, but no one had facts to support anything.

I scrolled back up to the pictures. Caterine and Ariane could have been models. They had been imprisoned for so long, and just as Zhilan did, I feared what they could become in the twenty-first century. They already had over a hundred fans on that one website.

A wave of my inescapable hunger rolled through me.

I called Grant, and thankfully, he picked up. Before setting out to meet him, I texted Zhilan, telling her that something had come up and that I might come by later. I had no doubt my wooden bokken would be waiting for me whenever I got there.

Under a clear sky with a large moon, I crossed Key Bridge and sat down beside Grant on a park bench at the west end of M Street in Georgetown. The university was up the hill to our left, and the Potomac River down the hill behind us. Grant wore his usual brown leather jacket, sitting with his legs straight out and arms at his sides, as relaxed as if he were on a couch at home. I folded my legs under the bench and shoved my hands in my pockets.

"Nice coat," Grant said.

I was wearing my new black leather coat. Grant's compliment was a bold one from someone who had said they wanted to bite me under my old one. I smiled briefly, wondering if he remembered. "Thanks for meeting me here. I couldn't go out with Zhilan again." A young couple holding hands walked past us toward downtown. I hadn't fed yet.

"Of course. What's wrong?"

"It's just… every night since I've been with Zhilan has been so depressing. Or at least they start that way. I wake up starving, and then I find a mother or orphan or anyone I won't want to kill. After I drink, I feel better physically, but mentally… it's just not what I expected. That's all."

Grant stayed relaxed. "Who do you want to feed on?"

My eyes followed a young man in a dark blazer and jeans, heading across M Street.

Grant motioned to him. "So why don't you go talk to him? Or just take him somewhere? You're strong enough."

"What if I can't stop myself? What I lose myself in some aspect of his life that makes me want him more, not less? Or what if I block out his memories from the start?"

"Could you live with that?"

The lion paced, stopped, and roared softly. "Maybe."

I expected Grant to lecture me on how awful I was, but he didn't. "Then have him. Love every second of his delicious blood. When you wake up tomorrow, find another just like him and do it all again."

"I can't," I said softly, hating the words leaving my lips. But why couldn't I? Because Zhilan said so?

"Why not? We're spawns of Satan. We're immortal and beautiful, especially you. Our bites are pure pleasure for the humans we *must* feed on to live. Assuming God is up there, he let us into the world, knowing full well what we would be." Grant sounded a lot like Caterine. Of course God presided over the world. I had seen that pure white light.

"Go get him, Erin, and if he's not interested, take him down by the river. I'll keep watch. No one will bother you." The man had gotten far away and would be out of sight before long. Grant continued, "It's your right. You're a vampire."

Bowing my head, I felt chained to the bench.

"Are you really stronger, or are you still that same scared little girl?"

The lion broke free of the chain, and I was across the street. The young man's shoulder bag whipped behind as I carried him past the bench and down to the river. I bit his neck.

Oh, sweet blood. Sweet curly hair, sweet scent, sweet man.

Phhhwoof!

The furnace roared to life. Heat began to build.

Carlos's blood flowed into the flames. I saw memories of his gym pool, and grew hotter. The flames grew higher. I squeezed his fit body against my own and understood how he had gotten it into such good shape.

I sucked, and the flames burned from deeper and deeper. God be damned! Gulp after gulp, Carlos streamed into me. I had his blood. I held his body. All I desired was more of him.

His heart stopped. My tongue licked cooler liquid.

I looked up at the bridge overhead. In my haste, I hadn't been paying attention to anything except for Carlos.

"How was he?"

I let his body slump to the ground, and turned to Grant. "Incredible."

Grant nodded. "Leave him in the river, quietly."

I did and watched another of my victims drift slowly out of sight.

"Let's go." Grant started toward downtown at human speed. I caught up with him on the sidewalk, and we headed back up the hill to M Street.

My mind raced. Poor Carlos. Cursing God had been

wrong, but sweet Carlos had been so much more wonderful than the last few. At that moment, he had been *exactly* what I craved, and I had gotten him.

"Tell me about Eure," Grant said.

"What do you want to know?"

"Whatever you remember. Zhilan told me part of your story, and I have some questions, but I want to hear from you first."

We walked around Georgetown and then farther into the city, avoiding the Capitol area, the White House and the monuments. I told him everything I could remember and judged at all relevant. They were the same things I had told Zhilan, with the addition of a few minor details that came back to me. My story took hours, and we stopped outside a park on P Street when I finished.

"Wow." Grant seemed impressed. A group of chatting people walked by behind him.

"Yeah, it was a close call for me down there." Among the things I would never forget was being paralyzed from the waist down. I could clearly remember the internal sound and sensation of my spinal cord snapping.

"Why don't you think any of the Spectavi remembered you in the cathedral?" Grant asked. "As you said, some had to be lying, like Dubois and William, but all the rest? That's a lot of Spectavi."

"I don't know. I've wondered about that. I mean, I'm ashamed of how foolish I was, but there *were* hundreds of vampires who really seemed to be meeting me for the first time."

"Right. And what did they all have in common?"

"They were Spectavi? Their religion?" James had said they were mostly Catholic, and those in the cathedral certainly had been. "The blood they drank."

Grant's face lit up. "Exactly, the blood. I've always thought there was more to that synthetic blood than we know. I've seen videos of tests where we starved Spectavi. They experienced a great deal of pain and became very combative, but nothing unexpected happened to them. I always wondered if maybe we weren't looking for the right things or asking the right questions."

"What was her name?"

Grant knew the friend I meant, the one he had mentioned to me before Eure. "Carla. It hurt to watch her dramatic change once she started drinking the synthetic. It nagged at me that something wasn't right about it, but I kept attributing it to the fact that she had made a choice in her life that didn't include me. But this? Hundreds of vampires forgetting you? Todd suddenly forgetting you?"

"Oh, my God." I leaned against an iron fence.

"Yup. I think Edmond was doing more with that synthetic blood than benevolently giving a choice to hungry vampires."

At that point, assuming anything but the worst from Edmond made no sense. "So, do you think if they stopped drinking it, they'd remember, that they'd go back to normal?"

"I don't know. I really have no idea. But maybe."

I pushed myself off the fence. "Do you know where I can buy a good sword?"

———————

"I'm sorry I can't help you. Do you need me to call someone for you? Is there someone that can come get you? I can pay for a cab if you'd like."

My eyes shot open the next night. I had been thinking about Todd constantly before sunrise, and memories of when he had become a vampire filled my mind. I pushed open my coffin lid and climbed out.

I wasn't meeting Grant until one a.m., but didn't feel like seeing Zhilan before then. I texted her saying I couldn't make it, but definitely would the next day. All she wrote back was, *Please be sure to.*

———————

I ripped his tie and shirt collar to the side and bit into his neck. He had been walking so confidently down the street only seconds before. He did everything that way. I drank on, loving my choice for the night.

Kyle was aggressive when trading stocks and on the golf course. He had no trouble telling his clients the precise amount of their money he had lost. He had gotten good at it, always adding that he'd earn it back for them, and that they should stick with him so he could. Most did, and he spent their money on his Porsche and designer suits. When he had stolen enough, he spent it on his house.

Crook! Deceitful swindler! My fangs dug deeper.

I drank and burned. I hated his lies, but they kept flashing to mind. I sucked more and hated him more. He knew he destroyed lives and families when he stole, but he didn't care. He thought himself smarter, better, and deserving of all he took.

I sucked harder until, finally, a chill in the blood. Kyle wouldn't steal from anyone else, ever.

———————————

Holding my katana in its scabbard close, I looked around at the other row houses after knocking on Grant's door in Columbia Heights.

Grant let me in and closed the door behind me. "All black... sexy."

"Wonderful. Jeans and a plain shirt for you? Shocking."

He could think 'sexy,' but I thought stealthy, agile, and powerful. A tight long-sleeve shirt, pants, and gloves covered me to the base of my neck in black.

He smiled. "They're dark enough." He pointed at a door at the other end of his living room. "This way."

"Are you sure we're safe here? Weren't the Spectavi after you?"

Grant answered while we made our way past his brown leather sofa and the rest of his surprisingly modern furniture. The flat television wasn't what I had expected from a thirty-three-year-old vampire.

"We should be safe. They don't seem to be concerned with me yet. I've never seen them trail me here, and I only got in trouble when a few of us went after the Spectavi who had killed James. He was never much of a fighter, and didn't resist when they caught him. They killed him anyway."

We headed down a creaky wooden staircase to his

unfinished basement. Grant pulled the string running to an old bulb, and dim yellow light illuminated the concrete walls and floor. "Things have actually been better in D.C. for Sanguans over the last few weeks. I think the Spectavi are preoccupied with hunting the twins at the moment."

Grant walked to a second bulb and turned it on. "I will have to move soon, though, once the surveillance system is in place all over the city." He slid a thick metal door in the floor open, then turned a crank next to it, around and around, until a steel coffin rose out of the opening. It lay horizontal, parallel with the floor. He kept cranking, and its top came off the ground. Eventually, the coffin stood just short of vertical.

"We'll have to lock him in here until the synthetic loses its effect."

It would be brutal in there for Todd. My own hunger came so terribly each night that I couldn't imagine a second night after not feeding. I pictured Todd as a frail wraith, starved and unable to focus on anything but the agony of his thirst. "How long will it take?"

"I don't know. And I've been thinking about this. There's a very real chance Todd won't be the one we get tonight. If he's especially important to them, he may be better protected than some of the others. We'll still learn what we need to, but can you handle that?"

I gripped my sword tighter. More waiting.

"Erin?"

"Yeah, yeah, that's fine."

I was surprised by the massive free weights and a bench

press on the other side of the basement. I had assumed Grant's physique was natural. When we went back upstairs, I asked him about it.

"I've always been big." He flexed an arm. "Working out gives my muscles an extra pop for a few hours."

"Does it make you stronger? I thought we were just kind of as strong as we were, that appearances meant nothing about a vampire's strength."

He motioned down a hallway. "The garage is this way. You're right. I don't think it actually makes me any stronger, but the girls seem to like it."

"And I considered you more than just a big brute."

He stopped with his hand on the doorknob. "The girls like it when I take them to the theater, too." I had apparently hit a nerve.

Grant went out to his garage, and I followed. We got in his black Ford Explorer and headed for the office building in Virginia that my old company had moved into. It was possible Todd didn't work at that location, but based on Eure's website and a few news articles that Eure had hopefully not bothered to falsify, at least some of my old coworkers might.

Like when we hijacked the truck, we parked a few miles from our destination and traveled the rest of the way on foot. Thankfully, the heavy rain we had driven through stopped soon after we left the city. Again, my nervousness paled in comparison to my excitement.

I shut my door quietly and slung my scabbard over my shoulder. Once I connected the strap to my belt and tightened it, the sword was secured diagonally across my back. It would take longer to draw than if it hung at my side, but I preferred carrying it out of the way.

The katana had cost a thousand dollars, and in response to a question from Grant, the man who sold it admitted it wasn't authentic Japanese steel. Grant offered to buy it for me, but I wouldn't let him.

"Who'd you drink from tonight?" Grant asked, while retrieving a handgun from the backseat of his SUV.

"No one. I don't know what his name was." I fired off a question that had been bothering me since Grant had mentioned his prey at his house. "Why did you lie to me?"

"Hmm?"

"About when you feed, that you don't kill."

"I didn't lie. I don't anymore."

"Oh. Well, don't you care that I do?"

"No." He shut the door and pressed the lock on his key ring. "I do care that you aren't suffering needlessly. You've had a tough life, but you're immortal now. You should feed on who you want, how you want."

Exactly!

"Let's go." Grant sped off, and I followed.

———————

"Knock out that light," Grant whispered, pointing at a two-bulb floodlight at the top of the four-story building whose wall we hugged. Not far across a strip of wet grass stood an identical building. They were both Eure's, as were a few others in the office park. The security appeared to be nothing like at their headquarters.

"How?" I scanned the offices nearby, as well as the similar ones across the road in front of us.

"Didn't you just buy a sword? Jump up there. I've seen Zhilan do stuff like that a million times."

I drew my sword and planned for a moment. After a few quick steps, I jumped toward the side of the building across from us. As soon as my foot hit the concrete near the second floor, I pushed off, aiming for a large recessed window on the third floor of the building with the light. Reaching that one, I tried to hold onto the top of the opening for the window. My foot slipped before I had a strong grip, and I fell.

I caught myself with my free hand on the lower ledge of the third-story window. The pointlessness of holding my sword occurred to me, so I put it back. With both hands, I pulled myself up and stood outside the window. I unsheathed my sword, jumped, and sliced at the light. I landed near Grant, in darkness, without making another sound.

"Not bad," he said. "I did think starting with your sword in hand was an interesting choice."

"You could mention that next time, you know."

"Hmm…" Grant crouched and peered around the corner.

I crouched next to him, to see for myself.

"That should be the one, five blocks ahead," he said.

The blocks were short, but we still would have had to get far closer to see if we weren't vampires. "What now?"

"We wait."

I took my phone off my belt. 4:18. We had a few hours before sunrise.

At four thirty, the first employees came out of the front door. I didn't recognize anyone, and they all headed in the direction of a nearby parking lot. A security car approached, so Grant and I retreated further into darkness. The car passed without changing speed, and we peered back around the corner. Another three Spectavi came out, then two talking with each other after that. I didn't know any of them.

A few minutes later, my old boss Mr. Oliver and his wife walked out, dressed in casual business attire as if they were leaving any day of work at my old company. Then came Todd and the female vampire who had been with him in the news articles I found while at Eure. They stood at the entrance. Todd checked his watch.

"Let's go." I started to rise.

Grant grabbed my arm. "No, there's too many of them."

"I have to get Todd." I'd do it without Grant if necessary.

Todd put his arm around the vampire I didn't know. He looked so happy, and so did the blonde at his side, but she had to be acting. Todd was being manipulated, used. I couldn't leave him there. I ripped my arm from Grant and stood.

Two white Cadillacs approached, followed by two white SUVs. Each couple got in and they all drove away.

"Not tonight," Grant said.

Todd had been so close. He had been well protected, but we would have caught them by surprise. I knelt back down, and we resumed our watch. A few other vampires came out of the building, then Sagar appeared.

"I know him. He's a programmer," I said. He was a really nice guy who we had hired right out of college.

"Should he know you?" Grant asked.

"Definitely. I talked to him at work occasionally, and I went to two small parties at his apartment with some of the others."

Sagar, still very thin as a Spectavi, walked toward the parking lot.

"Then let's beat him to that apartment." Grant sped back the way we came, and I followed.

Grant had parked close to the highway, so we hoped to have a head start on Sagar. He drove very fast on the way back to D.C., just in case.

A block away from Sagar's apartment, we sat in darkness, parked in front of a medium-sized moving truck on the left side of the street. Sagar's building was old, and Grant and I hadn't seen a garage entrance attached to it. A blue van passed.

"What kind of car does he have?" Grant asked.

"I don't know." I kept watch out the passenger window. At that time of night, traffic was sparse, but a van seemed unlikely.

I noticed headlights in my side-view mirror that weren't

getting closer. A small car parallel parked a block behind us.

Grant saw it in the rearview mirror. "Open the back and stand in front of it. If that's him, I'll let you know. Slash him a few times with that sword. Think you can handle throwing him in?"

"Absolutely." I was finally going to get to use a sword against something other than Zhilan or a light bulb.

Grant brought a pistol out from under his jacket and screwed on a silencer. "Go."

I went around back and opened the SUV's rear lift gate. Facing Grant, who remained in the driver's seat, and standing a little awkwardly to avoid a puddle, I drew my sword and held it low in front of me, inside the vehicle. My eyes met Grant's in the center mirror, and I planned my attack.

I heard furious footsteps. Grant remained steady. A man sprinted by on the sidewalk to my left.

The move I had in mind for Sagar was one I had practiced in Zhilan's basement. I just had to execute it correctly.

Grant's eyes went to his left, then back to the center mirror. He nodded.

The scent of sterile blood hit my nose as I leapt to the sidewalk and whirled in midair. As Sagar turned to run, I slashed across his hamstrings.

"Ahh!" He dropped to his knees, and red soaked the back of his khakis.

I stabbed into his side as he tried to pick himself up. Blood poured, and he crumbled. Hopefully, I hadn't cut too deep. With my left hand, I lifted under his arm and threw him at the open SUV.

Tshw-Tshw.

Grant's shots hit him in the abdomen. "Back seat."

I slammed the lift gate closed and ran to the door. Grant drove while I knelt backward with my sword over Sagar's bleeding body.

"Silver bullets," Grant said. "They should keep those wounds from healing anytime soon." He raised his voice and added, "I've got enough to kill you, Sagar. If she doesn't do it first, that is."

My old co-worker looked terrible. Blood seeped through the fingers of the hand he held over the wounds in his side. He labored to remain upright. "What do you want from me? I'm just a computer programmer."

I couldn't help sounding a bit hopeful. "Do you know who I am?"

Sagar shook his head. "A Sanguan? I have no idea."

His words stung. Fresh, familiar pain washed away my hope. "You've never seen me before?"

"No."

With my blade a short foot from him, Sagar bled the rest of the way to Grant's house.

10

When Grant closed his garage door behind us, he turned in the driver's seat and fired past me into the right side of our prisoner's chest. Sagar slumped further and clutched his new wound. Grant ran to the back and opened the lift gate. He wrapped his arms around the smaller vampire. Sagar didn't struggle as Grant sped inside with him. I followed a trail of red and the thundering sound of the two racing down the basement steps.

"What do you want?" Sagar screamed. He began to fight mightily when Grant brought him to the steel coffin. The wounded vampire managed to grab the frame and use a leg against the back to resist Grant's repeated attempts to shove him inside.

"I don't know her! I've never seen either of you!" Sagar picked the wrong thing to yell.

I moved just close enough to bring my sword to his throat. He stopped struggling.

I pressed the blade against his skin. "Get in."

Sagar let his grip come off the side of the coffin. The moment he relaxed, Grant threw him inside and slammed the lid. Sagar pushed it back open a crack, and Grant launched himself against the coffin to force it closed. Grant locked a clasp on the middle of the lid and then one near the top and one at the bottom.

"What do you want?" Sagar screamed. He beat against the steel walls. Grant turned the crank, and I watched as the coffin inched toward horizontal. The battering of vampire against metal continued. Grant cranked and cranked, until eventually the coffin lay flat, and then it sank below floor level.

Grant moved over the coffin and held the steel door that would cover it. "Why did you become a vampire?" Grant called. The bashing stopped. "Tell me why!"

"To help the Spectavi rid the world of Sanguans like you."

Grant slid the door closed.

"No!" Sagar continued to fight against the coffin, but the noise was dulled underground.

While I stared at where Sagar had been, Grant came over and grasped the top of my arm. "Good job." He squeezed, and my attention shifted from the floor to him. "We'll ask him again tomorrow."

———————————

I almost leapt out of my coffin the next night. My intention had been to feed first, but I couldn't wait to go to Grant's. Once I got to his place, the locked door rattled, but didn't open when I turned the knob and pushed.

Just as I knocked, I saw shirtless Grant through a glass

panel, sitting on his couch. He lifted his fangs out of the left breast of the girl he held. Brown hair reached down her lightly tanned, bare back halfway to the waist of her jeans. Her eyes remained closed while she slid her hand across Grant's broad chest, smiled, and fell back into the sofa. He looked startled, but didn't skip licking his lips to get the last of her blood.

I caught myself with my own tongue at my lips. I'd have to feed soon.

Grant pulled a tight black t-shirt over his head and came to the door. He unlocked it and opened it halfway. "Erin, I didn't expect you this early."

Still smiling, the girl found her crimson bra on the arm of the couch.

"I, uh, couldn't wait to see Sagar," I said.

Moving with a little more speed, the girl put on a gray shirt and a black fleece.

Grant looked embarrassed. "Sorry you had to see that."

"No, please. I mean, it's your house."

The girl threw a black bag over her shoulder and came toward us. She was tall enough to kiss Grant on the cheek without any trouble. "I'll see you soon," she said. Grant nodded and opened the door further. I stepped aside, and the girl glanced at me before lowering her head on the way past.

"Alice," Grant said to me, while I watched her go.

Only when she was out of sight did I follow Grant inside. "The same Alice you picked to take your mind off me?"

Grant locked the deadbolt. "Yes, but it's different now."

"Why, because I could get away?" I was curious, not angry or scared.

"No. It's just… it's different." He threw up his hands. "Come on. Let's go see Sagar."

The wooden steps creaked as I followed Grant to the basement. Of course, the difference was that I could defend myself against Grant, I thought. But seeing his strong shoulders, an image of him with Alice flashed to mind, and a brand new feeling came over me. I certainly wouldn't *mind* tasting his blood, but it wasn't the same craving that accompanied the need for human blood. If I took Grant's, he'd surely want mine, and *that* was a big difference.

Grant turned on the first light as he stepped off the last stair. I turned on the second while he slid open the metal door. Sagar immediately began pushing and smacking against the inside of the coffin.

"What do you want?" he screamed. Then he calmed down. "I'll talk to you, just let me out. Please."

Grant cranked the coffin above ground level. He pulled a steel strip on the lid near the top, and a slit opened. I carefully peered over and saw Sagar's forehead until he moved his eyes into view.

"You know me," I said. "What's my name?"

After a moment, Sagar calmly replied, "I don't know you. I'm sorry if you think I should."

I moved closer to the box. "Is it too dark for you to see me? Did someone tell you to lie?"

He blinked. "It's not too dark. I've never seen you before last night."

His disappointing words hit me like a tremendous weight. Then the hunger I had been ignoring deepened significantly.

"I see your cross," Sagar continued. "How can a believer in the good Lord torture another like this?"

Grant moved over the lid. "Why did you become a vampire?"

"Like I said last night, to be a Spectavi. Look, I don't know who you are; I just want to go back to work. I don't even really know where we are. Blindfold me and let me go. I'm obviously no threat to you two."

Grant slid the strip back over the eye window and locked it in place.

Sagar yelled, "I need my blood! Let me go, please!"

Grant began cranking the coffin back down.

Sagar resumed his beating against the box. "Please don't do this! In the name of God, have mercy!"

Grant slid the door closed. I walked upstairs and plopped into the corner of Grant's couch, where Alice had been.

Grant emerged from the basement. "Are you all right?"

"Yeah, I'm fine." In truth, Sagar's words had shaken me and brought to mind something I had been avoiding.

"We'll ask him again tomorrow."

"Good." I remembered the pure white light I had seen in the dark void. "Why did you stop killing the girls you drink from?"

Grant looked down at me. "Many reasons. For one, I started to care about their lives." He took a seat on the other end of the couch. "To most of the world, we're nothing but monstrous blood drinkers. Some understand us better, but most believe we feast on humans for sustenance, and sustenance alone. You know that we experience so much more than that. If we let ourselves, we can be closer to someone than a human ever could. We can know how they think, why they think it, and how they feel. We can know their hopes and their dreams. We can know someone layer by layer, to their core, but it takes more than one bite, on more than one night, to get there."

"What if I don't care?" I asked. "My own life is only a couple years old. What if I don't want to know the details of everyone else's?"

"So don't care. Do what you want."

"What about God? I saw the light of Heaven when I was dying. I know Satan's evil is what gives me life and compels me to feed my nightly hunger. If God and the Devil are real, shouldn't I care?"

"You said it yourself. You don't. And you might as well hear this tonight, rather than in five years, or fifty: whatever you think you *know* about God and the Devil, vampires much older than you *know* other things about them."

"But I saw the light. I know the twins' origin. It was Satan."

"You saw *a* light when you were dying, and I have no doubt Edmond knew his family history. Whatever transformed those girls was truly evil, but the name for that evil was 'Satan' because of their family's religion."

I remembered the massive crucifix hanging in Edmond's replica of Chartres Cathedral. "But the Spectavi are almost all Catholic. Surely among all those old vampires, they know some truths about God."

"I don't buy that for a second. That nearly every Spectavi is that same religion makes them more like a cult to me. People all over the world question their faith; none of the Spectavi ever do."

"The synthetic blood," I said, realizing how Edmond could have used it to control his vampires.

"Possibly. If a great evil had the power to give us everlasting life, I do hope some great force for good opposes it. I would never tell you what to think. But I will implore you to think hard before putting your faith into the neat box of a human religion."

I got up. I had to feed. Saying the word 'blood' had made my aching impossible to ignore any longer. "You're not just a brute, Grant. I've always known that."

He appeared pleased, and I headed out.

———

I killed another man after leaving Grant's. Before biting him, lingering questions about God and his adversary troubled me, but my focus returned as the man's blood stoked the fire within. I didn't let myself learn a thing about him.

Afterward, my first thought was wondering what Sagar must be enduring, and even more, what another night without feeding would do to him. If we were wrong, we were torturing Sagar for no reason.

But why did Sagar's suffering matter all of a sudden? Because he had pointed out my tattoo? I remembered something I had often struggled with as a human: the *Bible*—both Testaments—were written before the first vampires appeared in the world. While I had generally tried to live up to the ideals in that book as a girl, maybe that had been pointless. What good was a text that predated such an important change in history?

A lot of what Grant had said made sense. The worst part of my nights was fighting my guilt for taking lives. I hated the mental struggle afterward, so why shouldn't I just let that guilt go? The prospect of carrying it with me, night after night, forever, sounded unbearable.

I had been significantly happier before Zhilan showed up and started pushing me to care.

———————

Sparring helped take my mind off my weighty internal debate. While initially disappointed to still be using a wooden katana, I cheered up eventually. Zhilan and I practiced going a lot faster, pushing far past mortal speed. Predictably, the precision of my moves suffered. More surprising was how much I had to focus to correct those mistakes. After a few hours, once again bruised and sore, I found myself mentally exhausted as well.

Thwack!

Zhilan whacked me across my arm, and I stumbled.

She stepped back. "Has the boy told you anything about Todd?"

"Did you follow us, or did Grant tell you?"

"I followed you from a distance. You need to be more careful. You two could have been caught."

"We were fine."

"What do you hope he will tell you?"

"I went to get Todd, but Grant wouldn't let me. I want to know why Todd and Sagar don't remember me. We think it has something to do with the synthetic blood."

"At least you had the sense to leave Todd. They might not think much of Sagar's disappearance." Zhilan thought for a moment. "The synthetic does not do that. What you're talking about is too specific. It does seem to addict the vampires who are on it, like a drug they cannot live without. We have tested on them for years, and it's awful for them to stop taking it. Many have died far faster than they should have when we cut off their supply abruptly."

The disappointments continued. "Then, what is it? Why don't they know me anymore? Why did none of the Spectavi at Eure know me?"

"I don't know. It must be something else."

I threw down my bokken and walked toward the stairs.

"Killing humans will not make Sagar or Todd remember," Zhilan called after me. She had clearly followed me more than once.

I returned to my coffin early and lay with the lid open. If Zhilan was correct about the synthetic, that also meant it didn't have anything to do with the religious choice of the Spectavi. Perhaps I had been overly eager to jump to conclusions. Maybe I just wanted an excuse to feel okay about killing my prey.

Or maybe Grant was right, and I was too quick to already be considering brushing aside what he had said. I pictured the platinum cross Edmond had given me, tangled in my top desk drawer. What kind of god would let a monster like him live for so long?

My frustration and uncertainty built. The night would end eventually, and my maddening thirst would demand my attention when I awoke. Not wanting to waste the time before then worried about things that made no sense, I closed the coffin lid and imagined myself with Luke until falling asleep.

———————

"Please… please. I need my blood," Sagar pleaded the next night when Grant slid open the steel strip.

"We can find you someone to drink from, if you'd like," Grant offered.

"No, I need *my* blood. Please let me go back to work and get a little."

"Sorry," Grant said. "Why did you become a vampire?"

"I already told you." Sagar sounded defeated.

Grant stepped back, and I walked over. "Do you know me?"

Sagar's eyes had grown heavy. "No."

I closed the slot, then walked close to Grant and whispered, "What if we're wrong?"

"Then we'll let him go eventually."

"What if he dies in there?"

"Then he dies." Grant locked the opening and cranked the coffin down.

"No! No! Please!" Sagar screamed, but his attacks on the walls of his prison weren't nearly as aggressive as they had been.

Starving, thirsty, and damp from light rain, I stood in the plain industrial building where Shattered Nights had last played. I wore my old coat, but hadn't bothered with an umbrella. Even though the newsletter had proven reliable, I checked the band's website every night and knew that their next scheduled show wasn't for a while. I hadn't been able to think of anywhere else to go.

The band that evening was decent, but the persistent conversations in the crowd told the story. They liked the music, but no one felt they had to stop what they were doing to hear every note. The lead singer was no Luke.

I could see Luke up on that very stage, and wished I had followed him after the last show. Shattered Nights would have ceased to exist, but imagining his warm sweet blood pouring into me, I really didn't care.

A wedding band on a limp finger told me that I had taken my frustration out on a married man after the show. I hadn't checked before drinking. Kneeling beside him in the rain, I didn't know what to think. His wife would miss him, but I'd never know if any children would. I wondered if his parents were alive and I wished to have never seen the ring.

I dragged his lifeless body to a dumpster, then slowly made my way south to Virginia, and eventually, Zhilan's. Tao opened the door and led me into the living room where crackling came from a brick fireplace. Zhilan, wearing a loose pink robe, sat reading in the middle of her old red couch. She looked up from her book.

"How did you make it two hundred and seventy years without having your revenge on Edmond?" I asked. "I haven't made it a month, and I'm in agony knowing Alexander is still out there and Todd is captive." The next part was harder to admit. "Waiting is driving me crazy. I killed a married man tonight. I know nothing else about him or his family. I don't know what to do, or what to think."

Zhilan closed her book and placed it in on the end table to her right. "I did poorly, I told you. Rage is the source of your trouble and despair. I think you are finally starting to see that, which is good. I don't want rage to drive your actions like it drove mine."

"What happened?"

"Sit, please."

I took off my wet coat and handed it to Tao when he reached for it. He left the room, and I sat in a red-cushioned chair to the right of the couch. The warmth of the fire was pleasant, but after I glanced at it, I slowly slid away and scrunched tight against the chair's wooden arm.

"Will you listen to the whole story?" Zhilan asked.

"Yes, yes."

She smiled as though she really meant it. "Relax, Erin. I'm glad you're here. I just want you to relax." She let the smile fade. "In 1733, in Canton—now Guangzhou—in southern China, I was fourteen and still a human girl. Canton was an important port and trading city, just like it is today. Back then, much of the trade was driven by demand from Europe for Chinese silk, porcelain, and tea. One way

Europeans paid for the goods was silver. When they ran short of silver, they paid with the drug opium, even though the Emperor had outlawed it in 1729, because so many people had become addicted.

"Before I turned fifteen, my mother contracted a fever and died. It happened very suddenly, and I was so young that I had not truly appreciated my time with her before she was gone. I became very sullen.

"My father was a blacksmith, and after that, he taught me to use a sword because it was the only thing he could find that cheered me up. Between practicing, helping him with his work, and reading, my days were simple. An endless stream of ships came and went, but even in Canton, I didn't think global trade had anything to do with me.

"Three years later, in 1736, a group of Spectavi showed up, and everything changed. I had seen a few vampires before, but none anywhere near as old or important as Edmond and Victoria. Their arrival ushered in an exciting, hope-filled season before a long, dark storm.

"Canton was important to Eure for all the same reasons it was important to the rest of Europe: access to Chinese products. Edmond's plan to secure good relations with the city was to invite one family to become Spectavi. The family would move back with them to France for a time, and because they were vampires, a long-lasting bond between Eure and Canton would be formed. In a lot of ways, it was the business version of a royal marriage between two countries in Europe.

"Edmond and Victoria spent a few weeks meeting many

local families, including my father and me. I remember well sparring with Victoria, both because it was the first of many confrontations with her, and also because I did so poorly. My father had taught me bad habit after bad habit. Nevertheless, Victoria saw potential. She was imposing and reserved, just as she is now, but there was also a subtle air of hope about her. She told me that, no matter what, I should always keep practicing and that if I did, I could be great. After that, my father and I, along with one other family, began seeing the vampires every few days.

"Feng was two years older than me. His father worked as a government official, and his mother was a respected woman in the city. When we met with Edmond and Victoria for dinners or tea, Feng's family always showed up in finer clothes and carried much more of the conversation than my father and I.

"When we fought with Victoria, Feng was far better than me. He was a passionate, aggressive fighter and had been well trained. He was also bigger and stronger.

"I was in awe of the vampires, and also of Feng and his parents because of how well they handled themselves in front of the powerful creatures. I knew they would be the ones chosen. Compared to my father and me, their intact family seemed far more worthy."

Zhilan's smile came back. "Another reason I didn't really mind was that, on days when we didn't meet with the vampires, Feng and I started seeing each other on our own. He was handsome and smart, and very different without a sword in his hand. He shared my vivid imagination of what life as an immortal could be like. We would sneak off together and lay under the stars, making up stories about far off lands we would see with the Spectavi. My father had to have heard me going out night after night, but he never said anything. I could tell he was glad to see me happy for the first time in years.

"Feng promised that after he became a Spectavi, he would come back and make me one, too. With all the time in the world, we would make our stories come true together.

Her smile faded again. "Then, at dinner one night a month and a half after Edmond and Victoria had arrived, they told us all that my father and I could return with them to France. We were shocked, but agreed immediately. I will never forget the look of disgust on Feng's face before he and his family stormed off.

"I asked Victoria why she had chosen me and not Feng, who was a better fighter. She said Edmond had made the ultimate decision, but that I should not doubt that I could become a great warrior.

"For the next week before our ship was to sail, my father and I prepared to leave. He finished what work he could, and his other customers understood why he couldn't complete their projects. Everyone recognized the great honor it was to be chosen to be a Spectavi."

Tao came in with two logs and added them to the fire. As passionately as I loved the fire I could ignite inside me, the look of the flames in the living room worried me. I didn't want to be burned, but let myself settle into the middle of my chair anyway. Zhilan would have said something if it wasn't safe.

She continued, "For three straight days, I tried to say goodbye to Feng and remind him that I'd be back for him, but he would never see me. It hurt, but I still intended to fulfill my promise to him eventually.

"Then, late the night before we were to leave for Europe, Feng showed up at my home. He apologized for how he had been acting and congratulated me. We spent another wonderful night together. When loud knocking on my door woke me early the following morning, it was still dark, and I was surprised to find that Feng had already gone.

"My father answered the door, and police streamed in. I went out and watched them ransack what wasn't packed in our home. Before long, one of them pulled a large green bag from a cabinet drawer, checked inside, and nodded to his commander. The commander led my father away, and another officer held me back from them. 'Opium,' the man who held me said. My father swore it wasn't his and urged me not to do anything. He said his name would be cleared.

"I rushed to find Edmond before sunrise to tell him what happened, including the fact that Feng had to have planted the opium. Edmond immediately grew concerned because his ship had to set sail that night. He said he would go talk to the police before then.

"I found no one at Feng's home, so I returned to my own. The single longest day of my life passed. I was never allowed to see my father, and I never found Feng's family. Finally Edmond showed up that evening. He told me that Feng and his parents had denied any wrongdoing, and that they would be traveling with him now. Edmond offered to take me as well, but my father would not be released in time to go. I pleaded with Edmond to drink from Feng and know the truth, but he wouldn't. He said he couldn't risk damaging his business relationship with Canton. His honesty was brutal.

"I told Edmond I would not go without my father. Edmond said that he understood, and that he had received assurances my father wouldn't be hurt and would be held for no more than a week. Edmond apologized that the timing of the events was so bad and then left.

"I tried again to see my father, but the police wouldn't let me. I went to Feng's home, but he and his family were gone. By the time I got to the dock, their ship had departed. I watched as it, and my future, sailed away.

"I spent the night hating Feng and trying to think of a way to make him pay for what he had done. I hated Edmond, as well, for refusing to help, but Feng had been the treacherous one. He had been my friend, he had been to my bed, and he had betrayed my father and me. I vowed to have my revenge, even though I knew I never would.

"The next morning, a sudden knock brought me to my front door for the second day in a row. A young police officer dutifully and coldly informed me that my father had died in the night. I rushed to the jail and was shown my father's beaten and bloody body. The commander who had led him from our home casually apologized and informed me that my father had been unwilling to answer their questions. In other words, they tortured him, and they went too far. The commander had to claim it was an accident because he lacked the authority to execute a man.

"I returned home, crushed and alone. The venom I had been building up toward Feng and Edmond dissipated as the hopelessness of the situation sapped my energy. For a few days, I slowly unpacked our things. I imagined myself in Canton, grown, with a family. Back then, it seemed such a boring fate.

"Of course, that was not to be. While going through my father's papers, I found a two-year-old letter from Greece from someone named Houjin. It merely asked my father how he and his family were. Another letter from Houjin had come to my grandfather fifty years earlier. A third letter from Houjin had come a hundred years before that, conveying Houjin's displeasure with the Spectavi. It was a reasonable conclusion that Houjin was a Sanguan vampire with ties to my family.

"A means to have my revenge had presented itself, and I would take it. Feng would pay, and because Edmond had left my father to die, I despised him just as much. Venom coursed through me once more."

From my comfortable chair in Zhilan's living room, it was hard for my mind to accept that her story had really taken place hundreds of years earlier. It no doubt had, but she looked so young and calm. I became keenly aware that I hadn't worried about my own troubles while she told me of hers. I was relaxed for a change.

Zhilan adjusted her robe and continued, "I pleaded with every ship captain who stopped in Canton to take me with them when they departed. I passed on a few who obviously wanted me for themselves along the way, and eventually took a chance and made it to India aboard a ship sailed by a good man from Britain. I learned to be strong and aggressive at all times on that voyage. At sea, my dreams were no longer of trips around the world, even though I was taking one. They were of revenge and nothing else.

"I started learning English aboard that boat and was nineteen by the time I reached Thessaloniki, Greece. I had become a better fighter and learned how to act around men who saw me as nothing more than an exotic conquest.

"With fewer vampires in the world than today, leads at bars and dens proved hard to come by. Threats and bites were easier to find, but would not deter me. My confidence would not be shaken, and I spent every night in search of information about Houjin.

"It took months, but eventually, a vampire said he could take me to someone who might help, if I let him drink from me first. I did, and was brought to Alexander's castle. I was led past disgusting sight after disgusting sight. Men, women, and other vampires were chained to walls and locked in cages, all partially drained of their blood. No one struggled. All were resigned to their fate.

"Alexander was a big Greek vampire and was not yet disfigured. When we reached him on a dark metal throne, I was presented to him. He thanked the vampire who had led me in. Then Alexander cut off his head for biting me first. Alexander wasted no time and drank from me until I was very weak. I expected shackles and chains to come next, but they didn't.

"Alexander hated Edmond and the Spectavi, and

promised to help me if I would fight with him after becoming a vampire. He offered to make me one, and I considered it, but I had been searching for Houjin for too long to abandon my quest on the brink of success. I accepted the rest of his offer, and after being taken to Italy, met a man who brought me to a small house not far from Rome. With the sun high overhead, I sat on the ground outside Houjin's house and waited.

"At nightfall, the old vampire came to the door. He was short and young looking, except for his very pale skin. Houjin wore simple robes and kept a simple home. I swelled with pride, sitting with him after a search that had taken me across the globe, but I had more work to do.

"I explained—in English because our Chinese dialects were so different—what had happened to my father, and what Feng's family had done. Houjin was already hundreds of years old and seemed so wise. He knew Edmond well and knew him to be deceitful, but he refused to take sides in the war. Unlike today, a vampire could be neutral back then.

"Because of that, and because Houjin did not believe revenge was a worthwhile pursuit, he refused to make me a vampire. He said he would let me stay with him as long as I pleased and would even help me improve with my sword. He also offered to pay to ensure I got home to China safely, if that was my preference. But he wouldn't give me what I had come so far for.

"Exhausted and angry, I slept most of that sunny day. At nightfall, I tried again to convince Houjin to make me a vampire, but he would not be persuaded. I told him I was headed back to Greece and to Alexander. Houjin strongly warned me against going. He said Alexander was ruthless and untrustworthy. I became the one who would not be persuaded. All that mattered was my revenge. If Houjin wouldn't help me, Alexander would have to.

"As fate would have it, men with ships at the port in Civitavecchia outside Rome were scarce that night. It would have been wise to ignore the boisterous group that I did find, and ask about passage to Greece another day, but I was impatient. When the first man grabbed me and I couldn't break his grip, I slashed his arm. Four of his drunken friends rushed me, knocked me to the ground, and began beating me. I lost my sword.

"I fought back until one kicked my head hard and then another stabbed deep into my side. When I was out of fight, they left, laughing as they walked away.

"I lay there for a few minutes, bleeding and only half conscious, until a vampire lifted me in his arms. I tried to speak, but couldn't. The next thing I knew, the vampire bit, and you know the joy I felt, even with death drawing near. And then, I found myself lying on Houjin's porch. The vampire from the port had probably found my memories of Houjin and been afraid of his retaliation.

"Houjin brought me into his home and placed me on a rug. He knelt over me, bit into his wrist, and asked if I was certain I wanted an immortal life, apart from humanity. Coughing up blood, I managed to whisper, 'Yes.' He brought his wrist down and I drank. After that, I was a vampire.

"That first night, I promised Houjin I would stay with him for a year, and learn how to live as an immortal, with no arguments about going after Feng's family or Edmond. With forever ahead of me, it didn't seem like an unreasonable request from the one who had saved my life and given me such gifts.

"The next night, however, as my thirst for blood grew, the rage I had promised to put aside screamed just as loudly. The nights dragged on, and I listened to Houjin's teachings about the value of the human lives I lived off of, but my anger led me to kill many of them anyway. When Edmond visited the Pope in Rome four months later, I couldn't wait any longer.

"I didn't tell Houjin, and set out alone to confront the leader of the Spectavi, but I never got close. I killed the first few guards, and then had some success against a few more, but eventually was far outnumbered. I barely escaped alive.

"When I returned to Houjin's, he was gone and had left a simple note, politely asking me to leave for breaking my promise. I read his words over and over, ashamed to have let him down, but also disappointed for failing to get to Edmond. Revenge continued to dominate my thoughts, and there was nothing for me to do but join Alexander and fulfill my promise to fight for him.

"Back in Greece, Alexander welcomed me into his gang. It pleased him immensely to have a pupil of the incorruptible Houjin working for him. Alexander said he would send spies to look for Feng. In the meantime, I jumped at whatever jobs he gave me. In small groups, we attacked Spectavi and took out entire families of humans. It did feel wrong, at first, to kill some of the people and vampires and not know why, but I wasn't in a position to say no.

"Alexander kept me motivated by feeding me updates about progress in finding Feng, and eventually, each night of cruelty rolled into the one that came after it. All that mattered was my revenge, and when he told me he had found Feng and his family in France, I celebrated by sucking the life out of a newly married couple chained to a wall in his castle."

With a grave face, Zhilan stopped her story for a moment and stared straight ahead, likely replaying that night from so long ago. Without changing expression, she continued, "The next night, I set out with five others and soon had my revenge against Feng's family. I drank my old friend dry myself. He denied any wrongdoing until the very end.

"My half-fulfilled revenge proved dangerous because, having seen success, I convinced myself it was only a matter of time until I got Edmond. Knowing I couldn't do it alone, Alexander's crew seemed like the place to stay—at least that was my plan.

"Before long, the Spectavi started making things very difficult for Alexander and the rest of us. We had to leave his castle, and in the face of almost constant attacks, we stayed on the move. We lost many vampires, but got our share of Spectavi along the way. One night, a powerful warrior named Sofie killed some of Alexander's best fighters—and closest friends. Fueled by rage at the loss, Alexander defeated her in a long, grueling battle, but he didn't kill her.

"For three nights, with Victoria's fledgling as a prisoner, we ran from the Spectavi instead of fighting back. Alexander took so much of Sofie's blood that when he cut her, the wounds wouldn't heal. On the fourth night, she died. On the fifth night, Victoria showed up with a massive contingent of Spectavi, and we were routed.

"I learned later that instead of giving Alexander a quick death, Victoria decided he should live on, horribly crippled, and suffer for what he had done. She cut off his feet and dominant arm, and burned them in front of him to ensure they were gone forever. She cut off an ear and scalped him so he would remain bald.

"I fled all the way back to China. I didn't have anywhere else to go, and alone, I saw no chance of getting to Edmond. On the journey east, the weight of all I had done crashed down upon me. Feng was guilty, but so many other people and vampires I had killed weren't. I had stood by while so many were tortured.

"I drifted from night to night in China, without a great deal of purpose, keeping to myself and practicing with my sword. Two years later, I drank from an old man high on opium. From his memory, an image rocked me. Edmond was overseeing the unloading of a large ship in Canton. Edmond checked a crate and verified that the opium inside was satisfactory. The man carried it down the dock and into the back of a cart. The man walked around to tell the driver it was set to go. When he got there, the driver he was talking to was my father. My father was to store the opium for a night, then bring it to a den in the city. He had worked with

Edmond to smuggle the illegal drugs. My father was not innocent."

Zhilan paused again before continuing. "My father was not innocent, Feng was not guilty, and Edmond was more horrible than I had originally imagined. He had to have known of my father's guilt, and had left him to die while he sailed back to Europe. Likely, he orchestrated the police killing of my father to cover his tracks. He sacrificed him to preserve his company's trading rights in Canton."

Silence filled the room for a while before I spoke. "That's... Edmond was so cruel."

"Yes," Zhilan said. "But unlike before, I allowed myself to consider and accept the slim chance of success if I went after him. I decided that I would have my vengeance against Edmond, but that it would have to wait. I would live a life not defined by rage, but would continue training. Eventually, either an opportunity would present itself, and I would be ready, or Edmond would meet his end another way.

"I stayed mostly out of the war until the middle of the last century, when Edmond developed synthetic blood and began attacking neutral vampires, in addition to those who openly opposed him. I found Houjin, and then James, Francis, and others. You and I both know what happened to Edmond."

I pictured Sagar beating against the sides of his steel prison. "How can I just let Alexander go, and leave Todd?"

Zhilan spoke sternly. "Do neither, but slow down. Learn how powerful Alexander is first. Come up with a plan to rescue Todd that's better than showing up to his office with a cheap sword to kidnap him while he would surely resist. You are reckless, and it's dangerous. And killing everyone you drink from is also dangerous, for a lot of reasons."

"Then what should I do?" I sat up straighter. "I wake up each night craving two things: blood and revenge. You can't look at me and tell me I shouldn't drink blood, so please, don't try. But if not revenge, what do I do instead?"

Zhilan leaned toward me slightly. "Learn from me, and we will plot your revenge. Appreciate the fact that you have an endless string of nights ahead of you. Take your time. *That* is all I ask. It is what I failed to do. If I had taken my time, I wouldn't have Feng's death on my conscience, nor would I have to bear the memory of all the other things I did for Alexander. Edmond would still have been killed last month. Justice would have been served eventually.

"My rage drove me to do a lot of things, including taking many innocent lives. I know your hunger is painful, but calm down and take your time. Stop blocking out their memories when you drink, and you will keep learning. It will become bearable, I promise."

I left Zhilan's very conflicted, just as I had arrived. The idea of waiting a little while didn't sound like the absolute worst thing in the world. Todd would probably be fine for a few more months. And maybe Grant and I were wrong about Sagar and the synthetic. My rage might well have been blinding me to other explanations for what had happened.

A thought of Luke brought to mind the other aspect of Zhilan's advice—who I should seek out and how I should deal with my inescapable thirst. I considered Grant's pushing me to have my choice of prey and to do as I pleased with them. Zhilan had tried to pair my rage and my cravings, but as the notes of *Ember* played in my head, I didn't buy the connection.

11

Before going to Grant's the next night, I watched a two-year-old video of Alexander, posted by the same person as the revealing photograph of the old Sanguan. That picture was no longer online, so I doubted the video would be available for long. From the inside of the projection room in a movie theater, the cell phone camera produced a grainy result.

Bald Alexander walked down the aisle to the left of the seats and limped across the front row, where all the people had their necks craned up at the screen. A soft thud came with each step as Alexander's heavy, metal feet touched down. When he got to the last seat, he squatted down beside a girl. Before he sank his teeth in, he grabbed the leg of the girl in the row behind her with his only arm. Alexander started drinking, people nearby screamed, and the theater emptied.

Alexander finished with the first girl as the last screaming patron was leaving. The next girl, he bit all over rapidly, faster than the phone's camera could keep up with. When he was done, she was alive, but riddled with fang marks. Alexander must have had enough, because he snapped her neck and walked out of the emergency exit, just as slowly as he had come in.

His torture of the girl sickened me.

———————————

"We have to let Sagar go," I said, as soon as I walked into Grant's house.

"What?"

"We're wrong, and we're torturing him. Zhilan said that the synthetic blood can't do what we think it did."

"We need to give it more time. Zhilan doesn't know everything."

"What if he dies and we were wrong?"

"How is he different from the others? How is Sagar, the vampire, different from the person you surely killed before coming here tonight?"

"This is worse. This is torture." Grant had a point, but so did I.

We walked downstairs without any agreement about what we'd do. Grant turned on the lights and opened the door in the floor. Sagar made no noise. Grant raised the coffin slightly and slid open the eye slot.

Aggressively, Grant asked, "Why did you become a vampire?" No answer came. "Why? Tell me." Grant grew enraged. "Tell me!"

"Grant—" I started.

"Erin." The raspy voice came from behind the lid. "Erin Rose."

I rushed to the coffin. "How do you know me?"

"From work. From Snap Safe. You were Mr. Oliver's assistant."

I turned to Grant. "You didn't tell him, did you?"

Grant let go of the crank. "I swear, I did not."

I turned back to the coffin. "Do you remember yesterday?"

"Yes," Sagar answered.

"Why didn't you know me yesterday?"

"I just… didn't. I remember not remembering you. I remember our conversation. But now I know you are Erin Rose. What's going on?"

"Why did you become a vampire?" Grant asked eagerly.

"Please," Sagar said. "I'm starving. It's so horrible. I need to feed. Have mercy, I beg you."

"We have none of the synthetic," Grant said.

"I don't care. Any blood will do."

Grant bit his wrist and moved it over the opening in the coffin. The first drops dripped.

"Yes… yes." Sagar's voice became less raspy. "More… please… more."

It was a slow process because Sagar couldn't suck, but he got what he needed.

Eventually, Grant moved his wrist away and held the wound closed.

"Thank you." Sagar sounded stronger, but not all the way back. "I don't know why I became a vampire. I remember two Spectavi showing up at my apartment. They said I had to go with them, for work, but wouldn't answer any of my questions. We went to a doctor's office. I was injected with something, and I couldn't stay awake, and then… I remember being at work, but… I was a vampire. What happened? What's going on?"

Zhilan was wrong. We were right. Damn her insistence on trying to slow me down! Todd could be saved, and if Sagar had taken another night to remember, Zhilan would have cost me that knowledge.

"I have to go, Grant," I said.

"No." He walked over to me. "Sagar, we'll be back in a minute. I'm sorry about all this. We wanted to help you, and this was the only way we knew how."

I followed Grant upstairs to his living room. "I have to get Todd."

Grant's phone chimed. "It's too dangerous. Todd was taken somewhere other than home after work. It's clear he's more valuable to them than Sagar."

"I don't care. I can't wait now that I know we were right. I just can't."

"If we take him and they come for him, we couldn't resist them here. You and I couldn't resist them anywhere, if they come in force." Grant looked sorry to have to say it, but confident in his assessment. "We need to tell Zhilan about Sagar. She'll want to tell the others, and then she, or some of them, will help us. You *will* get Todd back."

"You sound like Zhilan." But I certainly didn't have anywhere I could keep Todd for a few nights while the synthetic worked its way out of his system. "All you two do is wait," I said, while Grant read the message on his phone.

"Even you will want to wait for this." He looked up. "I think."

"What is it?"

"Caterine and Ariane just walked into Tuscan."

"Wow. Why?"

"Dunno. I'm going to go find out. You coming?"

"I don't know. I want to, but what if they see me? I don't know what they'll think of me now." Being scared of going to the club sounded awful, but their hatred of Vera had to run deep.

"Hmm…" Grant said. "I have an idea."

We slowed to a walk the block before Tuscan. At its entrance, a steady stream of people came out, but a few also entered.

"No police?" I asked Grant.

"Soon, I'm sure. They're probably waiting for the Spectavi, and if the Spectavi know who's down there, they won't rush in without organizing themselves." Grant grew sincere. "You look very warm."

I tried to make a face at him, but my big sunglasses probably reduced its effectiveness. "I feel like an idiot. I hate pink." The pink wool hat was all we could find at a convenience store on the way. The six dollar sunglasses wouldn't have actually been that absurd—during the day. As it was, with the shades and the hat pulled down over my ears, holding my hair bunched forward and around my face, I was reasonably well disguised.

"Don't come," a girl said on her phone as she exited. "It's… they're insane."

A different girl ran past her into the club, and then a boy. Grant and I followed him. No bouncer stood at the entrance. The first floor was narrow and overlooked the level below. Music played, but it had been turned low enough to hear the murmurs of the people coming and going.

"Who's next?" one of the twins called out over the eerie quiet from downstairs.

The ancient French sisters stood next to a pile of five bodies, and had obviously had no trouble adapting to the fashions of the place—or the century. One twin's blond hair was straight. Her latex, charcoal-gray dress appeared painted over her thin white frame. Her long legs ended in matching ankle boots with huge wedge heels. The other wore the same dress in black, pumps, and gloves that went past her elbows. Her hair was up tightly behind her, so I couldn't tell the two apart with certainty. A crowd of people stood in front of them, leaving a few feet of empty space before the demons.

A young woman with short, white hair called out, "Take me!"

Grant and I moved all the way to the end of the level we were on, and had a clear view down and across the floor below to the twins. Even from where we stood, their red eyes burned bright through my sunglasses. I noticed a few other Sanguans watching like us—cautiously from a distance—and a few very eagerly in the crowd near the twins.

"Come, then!" the twin in black called. The crowd cheered. Cell phones held up high snapped pictures and, most likely, video.

The fair-skinned girl's strappy sandals made her tall and

matched her short ruffled skirt and the white corset laced tightly around her. She made her way through all the people to the twins. Shiny black fingers closed over her wrist, and the girl was spun around to face the crowd. The twin in gray took her other arm so both were held out wide, palms turned upward. Everyone grew silent, and only the abnormally soft music could be heard.

The girl appeared impossibly calm. Her smile was more befitting of one savoring the moment after her vampire lover's bite had ended than of someone soon to top the pile of bodies Caterine and Ariane had already consumed.

Instead of bending straight down to her arms, the twins lifted her, moved toward each other, and bit into the front of the girl's neck. Her legs dangled, and her eyes shut. Her face strained.

The sisters stopped biting, and the girl opened her eyes. Blood streamed out of her neck, down her chest to her corset.

"Please—" the girl was cut off when the twins bit halfway down her arms. With red still running from her neck, the girl's eyes closed again, and the sisters drank. They stopped, and blood ran from the two new bites as well. Tears slid down the girl's face.

"Please," she begged. "More."

The twins bit into her wrists, but not for long. They held her bleeding and red-stained body for a few seconds, perhaps posing. Then they finished her off with new bites in her neck. When they were done, the girl joined the pile. Most of the crowd erupted into wild cheers and screams. A few people slipped away.

I turned to Grant. "Evil."

He nodded.

The sister in gray raised her arm and made a fist. "Damn the Spectavi and their laws! Damn them for how they have hunted us. Brothers and sisters, we must not cower before them any longer!" The Sanguans in the crowd—but not those back near us—shouted in agreement. A few people did as well. "Men and women, they threaten our way of life, this way of life that you love. Will you join us when called upon? Will you fight with us?"

About a quarter of the crowd had left since the death of the girl in white, but the rest yelled wildly in the affirmative.

"Who's next?" the twin in black called above their shouting.

"Me!" a man said.

"No, me!" another woman yelled.

The scent of Spectavi preceded their assault. Along with the other Sanguans on our floor, Grant and I sped out while the soldiers streamed in. The Spectavi paid no attention to us, or the people who followed. We were outside and past the arriving police cars before gunshots rang out in the club. As we ran, block after block, I had little doubt the twins would get away.

When Grant stopped, I did the same.

"Their pictures are probably all over the internet by now," Grant said. "They'll be all over the news tomorrow. This was their coming-out party to the world."

"The people love them." I threw the pink hat and sunglasses into a garbage can.

Grant nodded. "Yup. Those two must have decided that the Spectavi have become so influential that the easiest way to bring them down is *with* human help. I assumed they'd stick to terrorizing Spectavi and humans alike. This could be even worse—for everyone."

12

By the next night, Caterine and Ariane had been all over the news—internet, TV, print, everywhere. One of the most popular images was of them holding the girl in white with her arms out wide and blood streaming down over her. There were plenty of other pictures as well, and lots of videos. That night would not soon be forgotten by anyone.

It wasn't that Caterine and Ariane had killed a few people, nor was it that they had done it in a club and called out the Spectavi at the same time. It was all of those things, and that they were stunning twins who had shown up out of nowhere. Put it together, and throw in the rumors circulating that they were very old and had escaped from Eure, and the press was almost as captivated by them as the crowd at Tuscan had been.

Public relations damage control from the Spectavi proved only partially effective. Their lies about the twins' true identities calmed the mainstream media some, but the masses on social networks didn't seem to be listening. Most condemned the twins for being murderers, but plenty claimed to support their call to end Spectavi "oppression."

More than anything else, everyone eagerly awaited Caterine and Ariane's next appearance.

Grant, Zhilan and I were on our way to Richmond to meet with a few other Sanguans to discuss the twins and what Grant and I had discovered. I only knew for sure that Houjin and vampires named Hayden and Giric would be there.

Grant and I had explained to Sagar what the Spectavi had done to him. Grant had given him more blood, and we considered freeing him, but decided against it until at least after the meeting. We didn't want the Spectavi to find him and know what we had learned. It should have felt barbaric to keep him in that box, but I had stopped caring. We were at war.

The limo ride with Zhilan was very different from our trip to the extravagant Fire and Ice. I couldn't wait to reach Richmond, and had become so much stronger than the nervous little girl who had been taken to that club. I sat across from Zhilan instead of next to her, wearing black pants and an emerald green sleeveless top. Grant followed on his motorcycle.

Zhilan wore a lavender Asian dress that she said was called a 'Cheongsam' and certainly could have fit in at Fire and Ice without any problem.

"You were wrong," I told her.

"I have never seen this before with their blood," she replied.

She had already said that she wouldn't help me go after Todd without going to Richmond first. She had echoed

Grant's warnings about the riskiness of kidnapping and then holding him. Zhilan used to seem a lot freer to me. "When did you become so cautious?"

Zhilan raised an eyebrow. "Hmm?"

"What happened to the vampire who danced in the darkness between bursts of fire? It was amazing, to be honest. Scared as I was of that whole place, I could feel the passion from across the club. But now? All you want to do is wait."

"So you want to go dancing with me?"

"No, that's not—"

"Yes it is." She spoke deliberately and forcefully. "There are a lot of things I'd rather be doing. I'd love to go out with you and dance with all the delectable mortals. You think you felt passion before, from so far away, but you didn't. You don't know the passion you could feel, and I cannot wait to show you, but you aren't ready."

After the discovery with Sagar and then seeing the twins, I had become so focused on the big picture. Zhilan brought me back to my own issues.

She leaned toward me. "When the blaring electronic beats make it impossible to hear each other talk, could you take hold of a man, feel his body against your own, and sip on him for hours? Could you let him take hold of you while listening to his blood pulse through his veins? No. You would bite him and drain him. You would trade a chance at real passion—maybe even real love—for a quick high. I am *waiting*, as you say, and imploring you to wait, until you learn to control yourself at a club, in front of vampires you think have wronged you, and in the face of Spectavi you underestimate. I have no interest in fighting alongside someone who would kill a girl to torture an innocent vampire."

"He wasn't innocent," I shot back.

"The girl was."

"So what? Why do you care?"

"Why don't you? Does that cross on your neck mean nothing to you? Do you remember when you were a girl, afraid to go out at night because of vampires like you've become?"

I pointed at my tattoo. "This cross is a reminder of a god who didn't care enough about me to save me from Edmond when I was Vera. The same god didn't stop Caterine and Ariane from becoming demons and spreading their evil by making more of our kind. He didn't stop me from setting them free. If *He* is even out there, and *He* doesn't care, then why should I?"

Zhilan leaned back in her seat. "Humans deserve better."

"*I* deserve better. My *life* was stolen from me." I almost erupted, but instead, finished calmly. "You could never understand what it's been like. Now that I'm a vampire, I will have who and what I want."

The conversation was over.

———————

After almost two hours in the limo, we pulled onto the circular drive of a large house with a brick front. We had to maneuver past a black Humvee parked in the middle of the drive. When we got out, Grant parked his motorcycle behind the Humvee, and the limo drove away. We walked around back where vampires in black suits stood at the entrance to the deck. Grant had explained that those Sanguans had agreed to a few years of service as guards in exchange for being made vampires.

Another vampire opened the sliding glass door, and I followed Zhilan in and through the kitchen. In the next room, a chandelier hung over a large rectangular table made of thick dark wood. It looked older and more ornate than the rest of the plain furnishings.

Alexander, sitting in the tall wooden chair at the end of the far, long side of the table, noticed us first. He sat next to a big vampire with brownish red hair who I assumed to be Giric—old and over from Scotland. Under his blazer, Giric's light blue shirt was crisp, while Alexander wore no coat, only a plain white dress shirt that was loose and wrinkled. He motioned with his one arm.

"Zhilan, welcome. Grant. And who's this? The one who set Edmond's sisters free? We're honored."

There was the vampire responsible for Kristi's murder. Victoria had succeeded in disfiguring him, but his voice remained strong and almost playful. Two vampires in dark gray suits stood behind him, both likely also Greek. One was short and had brown hair and a single sword across his back. The other was tall and had black hair and two swords. Zhilan had confirmed that Alexander was over five hundred years old. Presumably, his bodyguards weren't that old, but they didn't look especially young. Regardless, they didn't scare me.

"Houjin," Zhilan said. The small Chinese vampire wearing a loose gray robe nodded from where he sat the head of the table near Alexander. He was quite pale, but as Zhilan had alluded to, he couldn't have been very old when becoming a vampire in the thirteenth century. Two others facing Alexander turned in their chairs. They both appeared to be younger vampires, and had been maybe thirty-year-old men before that.

"Hayden." Zhilan nodded at the spiky-haired vampire wearing a black turtleneck. "Jerome," she said, to the vampire in a light gray suit. "This is Erin. She and Grant made the discovery we are here to discuss."

Grant tapped my shoulder and pointed at the chair to Jerome's right. I was still mad at Zhilan, but as I sat and she went to the other head of the table, I took pride in joining her in adding female representation to the council. Grant sat to Giric's left.

"Erin or Vera?" Alexander asked. "Caterine and Ariane, for all their power, and in spite of all the pain they inflicted on you, never imagined *you* would be the one to set them free. They hated you for so long for the experiments you performed on them, but after what you did, they had a change of heart. I visited them before Zhilan told us what had become of you. The twins were toying with the idea of making you one of us."

However virtuous my motivation had been when trying to 'heal' the two of them, I hated being held responsible for things I had no memory of doing as Vera.

"Ironic that their brother's blood had already done it," Alexander finished.

"They're psychotic," I said. "You should have seen them last night."

"Oh, I've seen the videos," Alexander said gleefully. "Those blond beauties were in fine form. With them, we will win this war."

Grant leaned forward to look past Giric. "We can't control them."

Alexander turned to Grant. "And why should we?"

"They'll bring chaos," Grant responded. "The way they incited that crowd, that's how they want to bring down the Spectavi."

Alexander appeared unmoved. "So?"

Zhilan spoke up. "Things could spiral out of control. The last time the twins walked the earth, gunpowder was arguably the most advanced weapon around. Now, they could do a lot more damage and kill a lot more people, much more easily."

"Who cares?" Alexander retorted.

"I care," Houjin said calmly. "And so do the others at this table, and many of our friends. Humanity has gone to great lengths to protect their weapons from being used against them by vampires, but Caterine and Ariane are an evil the likes of which no living person has ever seen. While his love for his sisters over the centuries was admirable, Edmond would have been wiser to put an end to them."

The room was silent. If Alexander had another quip, he kept it to himself. How could I have let them loose?

Houjin remained calm. "Grant, Erin, tell us what you have found."

I answered before Grant could, "I woke up one morning,

a little over two years ago, and I was no longer Vera. I tried to put my life back together as Erin, and then one night, my boyfriend Todd came home and claimed he didn't know me. After that, at Eure, I met hundreds of vampires who said they had never met me before. A few were probably lying, but most didn't seem to be. I couldn't imagine Edmond coordinating a deception on such a large scale.

"Last night, Grant and I confirmed that the synthetic blood could be responsible. It almost has to be. It made the vampire we captured forget me, and it also made him forget being forced into becoming a Spectavi."

"This is troubling news," Hayden said. He was lean and sat up tall. Zhilan had mentioned he came from Texas, originally. "This is far more specific than any of the changes we've seen the synthetic cause."

"It could explain even more," I said. "Like their religion. Maybe Edmond made them all join him as a Catholic."

"Perhaps," Giric said. "But perhaps not. The Spectavi followed Edmond to that faith long before this recent creation. What has become of this Spectavi?"

"He remains our prisoner," Grant said.

"Why don't we just destroy it all?" I asked. "We could go after the factories where the blood's made. When the Spectavi run out of synthetic, at least some of them would realize they became what they are against their will."

Houjin responded so quickly that he must have fielded the question before. "There are many such factories all over the world, so what you propose is no easy task. But even if we did cripple the Spectavi blood supply, what then? If we succeeded, what would happen to all those thousands of vampires? Who would the newly hungry feed on?"

"Who—" Alexander started.

"Edmond sought to wipe us out…" Houjin had raised his voice to stop him. "… and his Spectavi still may, but we will not be the ones to push the world into chaos that will lead to such catastrophic loss of human life."

I had never come close to thinking about it that way. "Okay, so what do we do instead?"

"We should find out what that synthetic is really capable of," Jerome said.

Zhilan chimed in, "Since we missed this development, it sounds like we need access to someone more important than who we have gone after before."

"William," I said.

Jerome responded, "That's easier said than done. William's a scientist, but he's no easy target."

I shook my head. "I mean, I saw William with something when I was leaving Eure. Before that, he had fled at the sight of the awakened twins. He looked terrified. But then, he went back for a silver case. A vampire in a lab coat brought it to him. I wonder if it's related to this."

"I could find him," Alexander offered. "The Spectavi are weak right now. Edmond's dead. If William is running from our beloved twins, and Victoria is busy chasing the two of them, this might be just the moment to go after him."

"He could be anywhere," Zhilan said.

"I have spies everywhere." Alexander seemed pleased at having been ready with the perfect response.

Houjin glared at him. "If you do find him, capture him. If you take his life, you take all he knows with him."

The one-armed vampire grinned. "I'll try to be careful."

"I'll go with you," I offered, picturing my katana slicing through Spectavi as we hunted for William.

All eyes turned to me. Zhilan said, "No, Erin, you do not need to go with him."

"I want to." Despite her insistence otherwise, she really did want to control me. I looked at Alexander. "If you will help me find Todd and rescue him."

He raised his arm invitingly and glanced up at the shorter of his bodyguards. "Kastor?" Alexander turned to the other. "Silas?" They both smiled, and Alexander turned back to me. "Of course! It would be my pleasure. Anything for Edmond's pet."

Zhilan stood up. "Come with me."

I shoved my chair back and followed her outside. Grant joined us and shut the sliding door behind him.

Zhilan motioned for the guards to leave, then turned to me. "Why do you want to go with that monster?"

I spoke softly. "Because I want to get Todd back, and then I want to finish things with Alexander. If going after Todd is too hard for me to do alone, I'll use Alexander to do it. It shouldn't be difficult for him to track down and capture one computer programmer. Then once he has, I'll be close enough to Alexander to kill him."

"Uhh!" Zhilan lost her composure like the nineteen-year-old she appeared to be. "Did you hear nothing I said yesterday?"

I crossed my arms. "This is different. Even you know Alexander was responsible for Kristi's murder."

"Not that," she said. "What about not letting rage push you to do this before you're ready? What about all those you'll kill for Alexander? Don't you care?"

We were at war, and if killing a few people or Spectavi furthered our cause *and* helped me have my revenge, that didn't sound bad at all. "If I don't go, will you come with me to rescue Todd tomorrow?"

Zhilan crossed her arms. "No. You are not ready, and I will not have my hand forced."

"Fine, then I'm going."

"What if Alexander kills you? Or you do not come back from a mission, or do not come back in one piece? Edmond's blood gave you great strength, but you still don't understand how to use it. You hardly knew yourself as a person, and you are a baby of a vampire. You first picked up a sword last week!"

"I'm no baby." And she knew my learning curve with a sword was different because of my previous training. "Look, I was clueless when I walked into Eure. I admit it. I didn't know what I was getting myself into, and I was scared, weak, and insecure. I'm none of those things anymore. I know what I'm doing. Alexander is dangerous, but I'll be careful. We'll get Todd back, I'll kill Alexander, and then I can focus on what to do about the twins."

The last part surprised Zhilan. "*That* is why you're doing this? Because Houjin scared you about what they might do? He doesn't mean today or tomorrow. He means eventually.

Those two have been alive for over fifteen-hundred years. You need to get your own head straight before you worry about them. I promise you, the twins, and humanity, will be around once you have." Zhilan let out a long sigh. "Remember how you sat and listened to my story? I watched the stress fall off your face, exactly as I had hoped it would. You were patient then; you need to be patient now."

I looked at Grant—not for his approval, just wishing he'd say anything to make the conversation easier.

He didn't disappoint. "I think you should do what you want."

13

His name didn't matter. My teeth sank in, and his already sweaty body grew hotter. Hot flame shot from his racing heart into me. His clothes gave him away as a runner, but I refused to learn anything else about him.

Damn Alexander! Vengeance would be mine!

I could taste it, and it was my right, just like the blood I pulled out of that man.

His heart stopped.

A dark green Chevy Suburban came to pick me up at my house later the next night. I had packed a small bag of clothes, my sword, phone, old coat, and little else. I wore all black, not knowing if a mission of some kind lay ahead.

A young-looking vampire with a crew cut drove. He said nothing except that Alexander had sent him. Recalling the fate of the vampire who had brought Zhilan to him, I didn't push for conversation. The two-and-a-half-hour drive to Harrisonburg, Virginia, gave me time to think, and I spent much of it mentally practicing my sword strokes.

Zhilan had spent years in search of Feng's family. With luck, I'd have Todd rescued and be done with Alexander in a matter of weeks. Before, as a human, I would have waited. I would have done what Zhilan advised. As I considered it, a life free of revenge had some real appeal. But I simply couldn't wait. I'd only be free of my quest for vengeance when it was done. That was what Zhilan didn't understand.

––––––––––––––

In the middle of a dense forest, off a dirt road, we drove through a guarded gate and into Alexander's small military compound. A grid of paved roads separated a few low buildings, and vampires in dark green uniforms manned numerous stationary machine guns on the top of the surrounding wall. We parked at one of the small dark-green buildings with no windows.

The driver showed me to my room which, unlike at Eure, was near plenty of others. I counted eight similar doorways on my hall, and two other halls like mine. The vampire left the sliding door open and walked away.

A simple black coffin sat on the floor in the middle of the small space. A partially rusted bathtub was in the far corner. A wooden closet stood opposite it. Rips in an old brown sofa exposed yellow foam cushioning. It was far from luxury living, but having my own room was a relief, and I didn't expect to be spending much time there awake.

I considered unpacking, but standing in yet another new bedroom, I would rather have gotten straight to the search for William. Loud, uneven footsteps made me hopeful I would get that chance.

Alexander arrived at the door in what might have been the same white button-down shirt from Richmond. He carried an old pistol in a holster at his side and wore faded black pants that ran down to what appeared to be old steel shoe guards, except they were his shoes *and* his feet.

He took a painful-looking step backward. "I trust your trip was uneventful?"

"Yes."

"Good. Come here."

I cautiously approached.

Alexander pointed at a mechanical keypad. "The six numbers you enter will be the combination to unlock the door later. Leave your coat, bring your sword, and follow me."

I hung up my coat and strapped my sword to my back, eager to finally test myself with it. I had no idea if the combination would really keep the door locked, but set it anyway.

Walking out of the building, I had to go very slowly so the old vampire could keep up. His strides were short lurches that seemed to take his whole body to complete. The loud metal on asphalt echoed while we passed two other small buildings toward the rear of the compound. It was very dark, with pale light illuminating some doors, but not others.

"Aren't you worried the Spectavi will attack you here?" I asked.

"Squad after squad of police and Spectavi have tried.

They've all failed." He didn't change his gait or bland expression. "I've also let the right people know that we have a nuclear weapon here, rigged to detonate if they bomb us from overhead."

"Is that true or just a threat?"

Alexander shrugged as we passed two banks of conventional missiles.

For a million reasons, the walk was nothing like my trips across Eure with Edmond. The reason I kept coming back to was Alexander's vulnerability without his bodyguards. I pictured my sword slicing clean through his neck. If I hadn't needed him to help me rescue Todd, I might have killed him on the spot.

As soon as I had begun to accept that the base wouldn't live up to my grotesque expectations, we walked up to the largest building I had seen. It was significantly wider and longer than any of the others, and at least three-stories tall. The exterior was green-painted concrete, and a few small windows ran across the top. Through a thick steel door on the far left of the building, we headed down a long, narrow hallway that extended across the front. The dark stone siding on the walls didn't match the exterior at all.

"The stone's fake," Alexander said, without looking at it. "It reminds me of my old castle."

We turned the corner, and a few last feet of hallway opened to a cavernous room with the same fake siding. Overhead bulbs provided minimal light to the spacious area. A dark metal throne stood three quarters of the way into the room, but a rattling sound took my attention from it.

Behind me and to my right, two pale women sat on the concrete floor, leaning against the wall, chained to it by their wrists. They were barely covered, wearing nothing but white underwear, and had fang marks all over them. To my left, a man stood chained with his hands above him. I guessed he was new because his brown loincloth left a strong and tan body exposed, and I noticed only one bite mark at his neck. He watched us as we passed. The blank-faced girls stared straight ahead.

We approached the throne on a long strip of black carpet, and I had plenty of time to survey the scene. Two men and a woman in blue were chained, hands over their heads, standing at the wall far to my right. What would one of the big men taste like?

No! I shouldn't have thought that. I did my best to ignore them.

Three women stood chained to my left. All were hardly dressed, like the ones near the entrance—one in white, one in black, and another in pink. It was disgusting.

I stopped before getting close to the throne.

Alexander struggled to climb the three small steps and slump into his seat. "I can see why Edmond was so fond of you and kept you as his pet. Did he make you put that cross on your neck?"

"No." He didn't need long answers.

"I hate it," he said. "What was his blood like?"

I remembered the first drops vividly, how they had burned my throat and then warmed every inch of my body. "Blood."

Alexander smiled. "How do I know you do not still do his will?"

"I don't."

"But how can I know? I believe you fled that place, and you may have earned Zhilan's trust. But as much as I would enjoy drinking from you, doing so would not reveal your true thoughts and motivations. You asked about an attack on this base. Our biggest risk is of a spy, someone getting to us from the inside. You will do something for me, if I am to trust you."

I tried not to imagine what terrible thing he might request. "Like what?"

"Kill a man. Not one of these. Find a man, bring him back here alive, and drink from him in front of me."

"Why?"

"Because you will kill who I tell you to kill, how I tell you to kill them, or you will leave. There's a college four miles from here. There's a small town outside it, if you would prefer someone older. You have an hour."

I looked down at the floor. That wasn't what I had signed up for. I had killed, but had done so to survive, to quench my dreadful thirst. The lion paced. Before coming there, I had accepted the idea of taking human or Spectavi lives for Alexander to help find William. I was prepared for that. Even without all the details, I could convince myself it would be a means to an end. But killing some local who had nothing to do with William? Blood didn't sound bad—it never did—yet I didn't ache for it at that moment. It would be pure sport to entertain a lunatic.

"Pet," he said.

Looking back up at him, I felt my heart begin to race. The big cat growled. I was no one's pet. Not anymore.

"Bring a woman as well. You should be able to manage it."

Zhilan had been right about one thing—Alexander was a monster. If I killed him, I'd have to get Todd another way, but it was a golden opportunity. In fact, maybe it should have been my plan from the beginning.

He added, "Hold the fragile creatures and drink from them slowly while they die in your arms."

My insides roared. I drew my sword and charged the throne with every ounce of speed I could muster. I swung down hard to end his despicable life with one swift blow.

Clang!

The crippled vampire wasn't there when I arrived, and my cheap blade snapped halfway up when it met the throne.

Chwak!

A solid steel foot raked across my face and sent me to the floor. I dropped my broken sword.

Chwak!

Alexander kicked me in the head again before I could move. My whole face felt broken. He crashed down on my back and wrapped his arm around my neck.

"Huuhh." I gasped for air through my mouth and presumably broken nose. My vision was a mess. I pushed myself off the ground, and the pain in my face started to dull. Alexander slammed me down again.

Still gasping, I leapt to my feet and tried to swing

Alexander off my back. He locked his grip tighter while I reached behind me in vain.

"You *are* still Edmond's pet!" Alexander cried. "But soon you will be *mine*!"

Alexander's fangs pierced my right shoulder. Intense heat hit my whole body. He was sucking my very being out of me.

I launched myself backward, and we crashed into the wall. The fake stone cracked, and the sucking stopped.

"Yyee!" the chained girl closest to us screamed.

"Ha! Ha!" Alexander yelled. He crushed my neck tighter.

"Huhh… Huhh." My head seemed better and my nose clear, but I couldn't force any air past my throat. I pushed us again into the wall, but hadn't produced the energy to hit it hard.

"Grrrrr." Alexander retightened his grip.

He bit my other shoulder. I burned once more. Vacuous space replaced the liquid that left me. My eyes closed. I fell to my knees. Alexander pushed me all the way to the ground.

He drank, and I ached for what he was taking. His theft of my blood dominated my mind.

My eyes opened, but after a gasp brought no air to my lungs, I closed them again. I felt so empty. How could he have moved so quickly? The world went dark.

My hunger bellowed from deep within.

I pulled my arms toward me, but only managed to move them a few inches. Soft creaks came from short chains that held them down at my sides.

I saw Alexander on his throne, halfway across the room, talking to two vampires—except I saw him through a thin rectangular opening. Metal was wrapped around my wrists, attached to the side of… a coffin.

Oh, my God.

Enough light seeped in that I could tell it was a coffin. My ankles had been locked tightly together and to the base of the box. When I tried to stand on my toes, a short chain prevented me from getting more than an inch or two off the bottom.

Shifting my body and straining my neck to the side to see, both the steel around each wrist and the chains running to them were at least three inches thick. My sword and cell phone were nowhere to be found. I remained dressed.

I pulled in with my arms as hard as possible. I had to be able to break free. I was a vampire! The chains held strong. My breathing had become very fast. The shackles felt heavy, but they shouldn't have. Almost nothing had been heavy to me as a vampire.

With her head at the floor, the lion roared. A chain around her neck kept her locked down, unable to stand completely.

Alexander had taken so much blood. The aching pit inside me called for my full attention, but I had to fight it. With all of my strength, I pulled in against the steel. The chains grew taut, but didn't break.

The vampires talking to Alexander agreed with something he said and walked away. Alexander glanced in my direction. "My pet, you are awake!" He struggled out of his throne, and I wondered if it was an act, or if he really had to exert great effort to move. Slowly, he limped in my direction.

Two men were chained to the wall behind him, so presumably, my coffin stood against the other wall. With that realization, I caught the scent of the women on both sides of me. It was faint, so they might not have been close, but I couldn't make myself ignore it.

I pushed in and out against my steel bonds, but again, accomplished nothing.

Alexander had made it halfway to me when I called to him, "What do you want?"

"Your blood." He kept limping.

"You've had it. Let me go."

"And your suffering."

"I'm not a spy. I hate the Spectavi as much as you."

Alexander stopped directly in front of me, inches away. All I could see were his blue eyes. "Perhaps you do, perhaps you do not. I'm no longer concerned with such details. You are nothing but my pet." He slid a covering over the window, and my world became black. As he limped away, his loud steps against the concrete grew quieter and quieter. Eventually, they were gone, and I couldn't hear anything at all.

I would die in the coffin. First, I would be tortured, and then, I would die. The lion roared, and then it whimpered.

My world was pitch-black whether my eyes were open or shut. My chains creaked a little when they moved, but that was the only sound.

I strained against my bonds, but they didn't break. I pushed forward instead of straight in, and then backward. Neither change helped. My ankles stayed pinned together and stuck to the base of the coffin no matter what I tried.

A few minutes of struggling exhausted me.

Sagar's sapped strength and raspy words came to mind. I tried again to break free.

———————————

Fool! Demon fool!

I woke, bound exactly as before, in total darkness. Why had I been such a fool? Why hadn't I listened to Zhilan?

"Alexander!" I screamed. No answer came. I ached everywhere.

How long would he keep me there? How long could I live?

"Alexander!" I screamed again. Nothing.

Thirst began to accompany the aching. Once again, trying to move proved futile. I couldn't ignore the fact that my efforts strained the chains less than before. I had gotten weaker. My fingertips touched the smooth metal of my coffin walls.

Approaching footsteps didn't sound like Alexander's. When they had gotten very close, the strip at my eye level slid open, revealing the dreary room. The bound lion roared. The two men chained to the wall across from me had what I needed. If only I could go to them. I pulled the chains taut, then started to cry softly. Why couldn't I have just a little of their blood?

Chains rustled to my left. *Mm.* A soft noise came from a girl in that direction. Whoever had opened the coffin's eye strip must have been feeding on her.

Mmm. The moan came longer and crueler. I remembered what she felt; I needed to feel what that vampire was feeling.

From where the sounds had come, Silas walked into view, in dark camouflage pants and a black shirt. He ignored me while leaving the room, satisfied.

I frantically fought against the chains holding me. Blood! I had to have it. I had to find a way to get some.

Kastor walked in, dressed like Silas, and headed toward me. He reached up to the top of my prison.

Cachot. It sounded like a latch opening. *Cachot.* He undid another at the middle, then swung the coffin lid all the way open.

I hissed in the face of the short vampire and continued to pull against the steel, contorting my body to try to help.

"Erin, how nice to see you again," Kastor said.

I hissed again.

His gloved hand shot out and held the left side of my neck against the back of the coffin. The tip of his index finger pressed into my tattoo. "I'm surprised he let you keep this, even for one night." He let go and turned away when the plodding footsteps of Alexander entered the room. "She's lovely," Kastor called to his boss.

Alexander kept marching to his throne, and Kastor moved to a girl to my right, hidden from my view by the wall of the coffin. I knew he had bitten when she let out a soft moan.

The lion whimpered. *I* needed that blood. Alexander's treatment of those people was so disgusting, but I would have drunk from any one of them if I could.

Kastor finished, and as he was leaving, turned back to me. "Mayumi is the one wearing pink, if it helps you imagine it."

He left, and for perhaps an hour or two with the coffin open, I starved while male vampires came in and drank from the captives, spoke to Alexander, or both. Judging by the weapons they carried, I guessed they were discussing nightly missions before heading out. Everyone noticed me, but no one else spoke to me or came near.

Then, the first female entered. She was short and wore a black satin robe over her very light skin. Black hair that matched her lipstick didn't reach her shoulders. She went straight for Alexander and interrupted his conversation. He brought a silver chain with a key on it over his head and gave it to her. She walked to one of the men on the other side of the room and undid the lock holding his wrists to the wall above him. With his hands bound together in front of him, the smaller vampire led the huge, muscular man across the room, toward me.

Step after the step, they came closer. I closed my eyes for a moment, but couldn't make myself keep them closed.

The man was deep bronze with messy brown hair. It was torture. From his chest to his abs to his arms and legs, every muscle was cut perfectly. My aching deepened with each step they took.

They stopped close enough that he could have reached

out and touched me, if only he would raise his arms. Instead, the fiend bit into his neck. He shut his eyes. She held his chest. Red blood seeped into the corner of her mouth and over her lips. It should have been my lips at his neck. *He* was what I wanted when Zhilan had me drinking from those wretches to make me feel bad.

For all the strength he surely possessed, the pale creature had to hold him up as she drank on and on. I strained against the steel that held me. *I* should have been holding him.

He probably wasn't even exactly what I wanted. I had grown too desperate to tell, but he had to be better than the ones Zhilan had steered me to.

The vampire finished with the man and spit some of his blood into the palm of her hand. She came close to me, and in a lighting quick motion, bit at my forearm, but she didn't break the skin. From the holes she had made, she tore the sleeve of my shirt wide open and smeared the man's blood on my arm. It had cooled, but still smelled like blood. She led the man a few feet to the left of my coffin. A lock clicked shut. I couldn't see him, but he was there, close, and his scent overpowered all else.

The female left. I looked at his blood on my arm. With my eyes closed, all I could do was think of him and my aching. With them open, the other man chained to the opposite wall tormented me. Why couldn't I have one?

Other vampires came and went. One in green fatigues led the humans, one by one, to a room at the right of the entranceway. My guess was that they ate there and were allowed to go to the bathroom. The compound had proven more gruesome than I had imagined—except it shouldn't have. I should have taken heed of Zhilan's warnings.

When a gang member departed and left Alexander as the last vampire in the room, he limped over to me. "Isn't he something?" He motioned to the man out of sight beside me. "He isn't allowed to talk. He doesn't have a name. He is just food."

"You're sick," I said.

Alexander ran his fingers through my hair. I turned my head away and moved my body down, but couldn't stop him from following. He touched my right wrist above the metal wrapped around it. "Soon, these won't be necessary, but you're a strong little one." He lifted me back up by the shoulder and bit into my neck near my cross.

I grew hot. A throbbing, aching darkness poured through me as he drank.

He sucked and sucked, and the darkness spread. He stopped. Red dripped off his fangs. "Well, you were a strong little one. Their blood comes back each day. Yours will not." He closed the coffin, shut the eye slot, and fastened the latches.

The pain and darkness persisted throughout me exactly as they had the last moment of his bite. Stuck in that state, I listened to Alexander walk away and out of the room.

Hours went by before I fell asleep. I yelled occasionally, but no one ever answered. I had been such a fool, and solitude before my death would be my punishment.

My skin had a slight gray tint when Silas slid the thin strip open the next night. It was another unnatural first as a vampire. I surveyed the room and ached. My throat had become completely parched. I was so weak and empty. My bone-dry eyes itched incessantly.

Just a few drops, I thought. With just a tiny bit of one of those people's blood, perhaps I could break free.

The man closest to me became impossible to ignore. I stretched my back and neck to bring my head down and my tongue to my arm to lick the blood that had been wiped on it. I couldn't reach. I tried again and didn't come close. I felt like an animal.

Silas walked to the far wall and bit into a girl. My aching burst into rolling pain. As she moaned and he drank, the agony moved from one part of my body to another, never stopping until he left and the deep aching returned.

Kastor visited me next. He opened the coffin as he had the night before and touched my neck. His fingers ran over my broken skin. "See, I knew he'd do something about this cross." Alexander's bite mark must not have healed.

My voice came out hoarse when I pleaded, "Help me."

He stepped back and looked me over.

I sensed a glimmer of hope. "Bite me, have my blood, and then help me."

Kastor smiled. "Alexander would never forgive me." He drank from Mayumi, and once again, my aching became a terrible, rolling pain.

The female who had locked the big man beside me returned, bringing another vampire with her. They were both dressed in leather—one black, one dark purple—with knives and guns strapped all over their bodies. The man made two low grunts as each bit into him.

When Alexander approached, a short, thin vampire in a white lab coat walked alongside him. As they neared me, the new one reached inside his coat and took out something sharp.

"It's hard for me to get all that hair out of the way with one arm," Alexander said.

The new vampire came close and opened his scissors. I turned my head to the side and dropped my body lower in the coffin.

Alexander picked me up by the neck and held me steady. I should have been able to fight against his lone arm, but I had grown far too weak.

Snip. A chunk of my brown hair fell to my feet.

I closed my eyes.

Snip, snip. He kept cutting while Alexander held me. My eyes watered. I loved my hair. Since the morning I had woken up as Erin for the first time, I had always had long hair.

My head was pulled forward.

Snip, snip. Snip, snip. Snip, snip. Snip, snip.

"All done," the barber said. I felt the ends of my hair near the bottom of my cheeks and just as high all the way around the back of my newly exposed neck.

"Thank you." Alexander turned to the other vampire and tugged on the bottom of my shirt. "And this."

The dull side of the scissors pressed gently on my

abdomen as the sharp edges snipped their way up my shirt. The vampire in white avoided my black sports bra and cut down my sleeves. My shirt fell to the floor behind me.

Alexander bowed his head slightly to the other vampire, who walked away. "Now, that's better." He made two sets of new fang marks over my cross.

He shut the coffin earlier that night, and I spent hours in darkness that matched what I felt inside. While weeping, I scratched at the steel walls with my fingernails. At first, the sound sent chills up my spine. But I got used to it, and then it became something to do to distract me from my aching.

"God?" I whispered when that distraction grew old. No answer came, and I scratched at the walls again.

Zhilan's words came back to me. "In 1733, in Canton—now Guangzhou—in southern China..." I hadn't heeded her warnings, but could retell myself her story for the sake of my sanity.

———————

Luke finished singing, and the crowd went wild. At the end of the show, a woman ran to him. They embraced. I tried to run and take him for myself, but I was paralyzed. I stood, helpless to do anything but watch them kiss.

My eyes opened slowly the following night. The lion had grown thin and sickly. She was so weak, chained to the ground, out of fight.

The vampires rolled in as usual. The same ones taunted me. I wondered who would live longer, me or the man beside me who made new blood each day.

When Alexander approached my open coffin, he wore a wide smile. My missing shirt was bad enough, but I felt even more naked without my long hair.

Somehow, I found the energy to speak. "Wha—" But I stopped when it hurt my parched throat to make the sounds.

"Shh. Shh…" Alexander pretended to feel badly. "I have news that might interest you. We found William. We only held him for a few hours before my troops were overwhelmed by Spectavi and he escaped, but in that time, he shared one particularly interesting piece of information." Alexander paused, as if to find a way to drag it out longer. "He told us what he had in the briefcase that night at Eure."

I struggled to focus on his words while wondering how much blood could possibly be left in me for Alexander to take.

He continued gleefully. "As you discovered, the Spectavi have made impressive advances with their synthetic blood. Once we told William we already knew that, he was willing to buy himself some time by telling us more. My vampires can be very persuasive." Alexander paused again. "William confirmed that they know how to induce specific, individual changes using their blood. Of course, that wasn't new. What I found fascinating was that it seems they've figured out how to make those individual changes permanent."

Todd.

"William carried the first batch of the additive the night you fled Eure."

"Please…" It tore my throat to whisper. Pulling on the bonds that held me was useless.

"Shh… I know you may not care that thousands of Spectavi will forget Vera forever. But what about… Todd, was his name? That would be such a shame. Before he escaped, William mentioned that the additive should be reaching the Spectavi blood supply today or tomorrow. It is unfortunate, because I don't think I will find the time to share this information with anyone for at least a few weeks."

Todd would forget me forever if I didn't get to him. It might already have been too late.

With the speed he had shown when he captured me, Alexander launched his fangs at my neck. The expected heat spread, but quickly became overshadowed by the doom of my blood trickling out of me.

He bit again, into a slightly different spot, very briefly. My neck must have been a mess of unhealed wounds.

When Alexander left, I could do nothing but stare at the closed lid and think of Todd. Maybe God was punishing me for all lives I had taken—including Christopher's. Or maybe he was punishing me for letting the twins free before that, or not choosing Heaven in the first place.

It didn't seem right. Or it didn't seem fair. What kind of god would give me such a choice at my death, only so I could fail to make the right one? Hadn't God put me through enough already as both Vera and Erin?

Damn him! He was cruel, crueler than even Edmond had been.

My single regret was not being patient instead of attacking Alexander.

The next night brought more of the same torture. Alexander drank just a little of my blood. I must not have had much more in me.

My vampire body could withstand far more than a mortal's could. As I continued to wither, and struggled to remember the taste and the texture of warm blood, I never forgot the fire that came with each drink, and how I adored it. The risk of the profound pain I was in was one price of that inhuman pleasure.

By the time Alexander shut the coffin lid, my head and body had slumped down to the left. Holding myself up had become too difficult. I tried to find some energy to pull against my chains—but stopped. My body persisted in crying out to be fed—unrelenting, unending waves of hunger screamed for attention—but my mind had accepted the hopelessness of the situation.

When my last trace of resistance died, shame settled in to take its place. The vampire I longed to be would never give up. I had come back to the world to be strong, to learn who I had been, and to right the wrongs that had been committed against me. In spite of all Satan had given me, I would discover no more about Vera and fall far short of completing my revenge.

I asked God to forgive me for failing Todd.

Living with the knowledge that Todd was lost became an additional kind of pain. If I hadn't come to Alexander's, or simply hadn't rushed to attack him, Alexander probably would have reported on what William had told him. We could have tried to rescue Todd that very night. By then, I might have learned about Alexander's secret speed.

Over the next two nights, I grew closer and closer to death, with no idea how close I was. Zhilan had been right to call me a baby of a vampire. I was clueless.

I asked God to forgive me for being so foolish. The prayer was painfully familiar to me. I wished over and over to have listened to Zhilan. She had been right about everything. I held no hard feelings toward Grant for his encouragement, even though some of it had led me here. I never would have listened to Zhilan. I never could have been humbled by her words alone. Only after experiencing what Grant pushed me to do, or chose not to dissuade me from, did Zhilan's instruction resonate.

I apologized to God for having taken innocent lives. I cried softly while remembering them. Paul, Anthony, Toby, Craig… the list went on, and the faces included all those whose names I had refused to learn. If only I could see the pure white light one more time. I didn't think I ever would unless God forgave me before my death in the coffin.

When Silas and Kastor came in on the following night and drank from those near me, I no longer sought to be the vampire at the girls' necks. As much as a single drop of blood could have made me feel better, the torture was all wrong. And while I had never treated anyone like Alexander's gang did, killing innocent people outside of his lair wasn't any better. My murders happened quicker, but they were still murders.

Kastor left. Alexander took his nightly taste and sealed my coffin.

In the darkness, I realized that if those despicable vampires were able to let their prisoners live, night after night, I had to possess that ability as well. I had considered myself so powerful, but weakness had led me to kill. Compared to my time at Eure, I had been a different kind of fool, but once again, I had been a fool.

"God, I'm so sorry," I whispered to the metal in front of me. I had killed all those people because giving in to the satanic evil coursing through me had been easier than being strong and showing restraint. Finally, I understood that while a potent evil had made me a demon, I had a choice. That choice was what the hell of Alexander's had shown me.

Alexander's demons had made their choice out of convenience, a fondness of torture, or both. If I ever got free, I would make my choice because I knew the difference between right and wrong. The people chained to the walls around me were treated as nothing but food, and that wasn't right. As a vampire, I needed their blood, but I didn't have to kill them for it.

Satisfaction or pride should have accompanied finding my way to such a significant understanding. Pain and the ever-advancing specter of death, robbed me of any hint of either reward.

14

The next night, after all the vampires came and went and I had been drunk from, I drifted in and out of consciousness for hours. It was impossible to tell the time, but at least being unconscious often would make the nights until my death pass more quickly.

Cachot. Cachot.

The latches on the coffin were undone. The lid opened, and the blurry image of a tall figure draped in a black hood and cloak stood before me. Pale white hands stood out in the barely moonlit room.

The figure knelt and—*crrack*—*crrack*—the steel holding my ankles was ripped apart.

Crrack. The vampire freed my left wrist—*crrack*—and then my right. I fell forward into leather covering a strong female body. With her arm around my waist, she carried me to the entranceway, and then stopped. She raced us back to near Alexander's throne.

"Victoria." The voice came from behind us, down the hall leading into the big room. "How does it feel to be the hunted for a change?" The voice belonged to either Caterine or Ariane.

Victoria?

The Spectavi warrior threw back her hood and kept hold of me while we turned to see the twin, alone in the entranceway. Victoria had two swords on her back and might have been able to take whichever twin stood there, but her sister had to be close.

And what was Victoria doing there?

"Or should I say the lured and trapped?" the evil Sanguan asked. "When Alexander told us that he had captured traitorous Vera, we hoped she would be sufficient to bait you."

The lights turned on, very dim, but slowly brightening. The twin walked in, and Alexander came from behind her, as did her sister, Silas, and Kastor. They spread away from the entrance, and eight or ten Spectavi dressed in gray marched in with their hands bound behind their backs in massive steel shackles. At gunpoint, they were followed by roughly the same number of Alexander's soldiers in green.

The chain of Alexander's flail rattled when he lifted it. "Victoria, you will be Vera's next unwitting victim. I was afraid after Edmond's demise that you wouldn't care to come for her."

Or after she had broken my body, bone by bone, punched in my lungs and paralyzed me, I thought.

"I didn't want you killing another of my daughters," Victoria said. "I should have ended you in Greece."

Daughter? Rivaling my pain, weakness, and shock, a profound comfort crept over me for the first time. I hadn't even been sure Victoria knew I had survived her attack on me at Eure. But she had come, and claimed to care for me in a way that I had never known anyone to care before.

She let me go and ripped off her cloak all at once. I glanced up at her, and while the cloth fell to the ground, her head and eyes motioned to the wall.

Settling on an opinion of Victoria would have to wait. I raced in that direction, pleading with myself to have the strength to accomplish what she asked, but only made it halfway before falling. The frail hands attached to my worn wrists barely braced me before I hit the concrete floor.

Ariane stood over me while I stared at the muscular man chained next to where I had been. "Are you thirsty, young one? Would you like one final drink before you die?"

I crawled toward the man, toward my salvation. He was so close.

"Have him," Ariane said. She picked me up under the arms. "When my sister and I dreamed of killing you during the last few excruciating years in those steel boxes, we dreamed of drinking you dry." She started walking while holding me. "Alexander came close to depriving us of that dream, but this way, we will all get what we want."

She threw me the rest of the way, and I fell to the ground at the man's feet. I glanced up to find him looking down at me, expressionless. I bit his filthy ankle.

The lion stirred.

Thump-thump.

My heart beat louder than the man's I drank from. Almost like the sensation of individual drops of blood running into James's mouth the first time I was bitten, I experienced the liquid reaching each of my cells. My arid, parched body began to consume the fuel. I grew stronger and sucked harder. I pulled Keith's blood into me, and the aching void began to fill—it became smaller and smaller, shallower and shallower.

Keith had met one of Alexander's vampires at a high-end lounge. She drank from him and tricked him into going with her.

I wrapped my hands around his calf and kept sucking. The void disappeared. I thanked God for the blood.

Keith was single… and so strong. He had just bought more weight for the bench press in his apartment. He was mine. All mine!

I ripped my fangs out of him. The man's eyes stayed closed; his head lay limp to the side. I had taken too much.

"I'm so sorry," I whispered, no longer struggling to speak.

Keith's eyes opened, and he gasped for a breath. Thank God.

I got to my feet slowly. I needed more. I could hold his muscular body while drinking more, but he'd die. It took all my strength to tear my gaze from him and turn to Ariane and the rest of the crowd who had watched me nearly kill Keith.

Victoria nodded at the wall to the left of my coffin. "Why didn't you kill William when he was your prisoner?" Victoria asked Alexander. She was obviously buying me time.

I raced to Mayumi. She looked terrified. The nearest unbroken skin to her neck was on her shoulder, under her right bra strap. I moved it aside and bit. Soft, thin blood ran into me. I couldn't remember the texture of Keith's, but had the sense to appreciate hers.

Glorious heat intensified as I drank.

Vvvvwwooosh! There it was! The furnace lit. Fresh liquid streamed down my throat into the fire. I sucked, and power came back into my body. The lion thrashed its head from side to side, and the chain around its neck shattered and fell to the ground.

My fangs came out of her, less than an inch. Mayumi struggled against the shackles that held her to the wall.

Her husband had taken her back twice after she cheated on him.

I spent a few breaths thinking it over, then bit back in, hard.

Roaarrr!

The third time Mayumi's husband caught her, he divorced her. But her family had more money, and they hated her husband. She hired better lawyers than he could afford. They twisted the facts and left him with almost nothing.

I gulped down soft blood until her heart stopped. *She* was left with nothing, while her ex-husband lived on—and so did I.

The lion stood proud.

Letting Mayumi go, I turned to find a few guns pointed at me, but everyone else focused on the conversation between Victoria and Alexander. Ariane had moved to stand beside her sister. I looked myself over. A shirt would have been nice, but aside from that and my newly cut hair, I appeared fine. Alexander's bite marks were gone.

Bastard! Oh, how I wanted to make him and his despicable thugs pay for what they had done to me. While walking to Victoria, I pictured myself racing from one to the next, ripping heads and limbs off with my bare hands as I went. The lion would have a feast. The guns moved from me to the other Spectavi.

"Feeling better?" Caterine asked.

I'd suck them all dry. Victoria could have the twins, but if I rushed Alexander, he wouldn't surprise me again. Kastor and Silas didn't look so tough. But I planted my feet firmly next to my rescuer. The warrior who had fought in the Crusades, and had been fighting since then, should make our next move, not me.

Victoria unsheathed the smaller of the two swords on her back. "Your katana. You used to be pretty good with it."

I took the top of the leather-wrapped handle in my right hand, and positioned my left around the bottom. The slightly curved blade gleamed from its point down to the electric blue collar at the rounded hand guard. The sword weighed nothing, and taking hold of it felt more natural than almost anything I had ever done.

I hated myself for my mistakes. I literally held a piece of my lost past, moments from fighting alongside one who had raised me and seemed to care for me again, but my stupidity would kill us both.

"Any gifts for the rest of us, Victoria?" Then, Alexander's smile faded, and he yelled, "Fire!"

His vampires gunned down the group of Spectavi prisoners. Victoria and I split up before they turned to us.

Bullets whizzed by and into the fake stone walls as we raced around the large room. The twins rushed after their old adversary, and everyone else came after me. If death was still coming, it was a far better death than I had been facing. I would fight to my last drop of blood, instead of withering away without it. If nothing else, I'd get the chance to see if I was as good as I thought with a blade.

Amid screams from humans, a bullet grazed my arm and another, my side. I moved quickly and erratically to try to avoid more. I was pleased with how our opponents had divided, but it soon became obvious that I couldn't really do much fighting. Victoria's longsword clanged against the twins' katanas, but there were too many for me to engage for long. Silas fought with two straight swords, and Kastor had a katana of his own. Alexander swung his flail at me repeatedly. Gunshots came less frequently as the others closed in on me.

Near his throne, Alexander caught a little of my thigh on his way to slamming his flail into the metal seat. Silas got me in the side because his two-sword fighting style confused me, but I started figuring it out. The wounds weren't bad and healed quickly.

Zhilan burst from the hallway and nearly sliced off Alexander's head with her straight sword, but he ducked to avoid it. The fighting stopped.

"Treachery!" Alexander yelled. "She's not one of us!"

Grant raced in, jacket open, assault rifle firing. "She is. You aren't!" He hit a few of Alexander's troops in green before they fired back and the fighting resumed. Hayden took out a few more soldiers and then sped his katana to Victoria's side.

Zhilan danced between Silas's two blades and Alexander's wild attacks. I finally had a fair fight against one of the animals who had tormented me night after night.

I cut—*tyn!*—Kastor's steel blocked mine.

He cut—*tyn!*—I blocked.

We shuffled forward and backward, our swords meeting high and low and side to side. He was fast. I thought I could be faster. Pushing myself to find out, I strung together one combination of quick cuts after another.

Kastor seemed surprised. "Not bad, young one. Not bad." Our blades met. "But we are not sparring." Our blades met again, then a kick to my stomach sent me flying to the ground. Kastor raced to me and slashed down, but I flipped over backward out of the way, landing on my feet.

I ducked under his next cut and spotted an opening. I swung hard on my way back up.

Kastor avoided it, and as my sword continued far past where he had been, he slashed deep into my left shoulder.

"Ahh!" I winced. Why had I wasted the effort? What a pointlessly long swing! I knew I could do better.

My left hand dragged through the motions while I fought defensively with an almost useless, weak arm. I parried blow after blow and shuffled backward, urging the gash in my shoulder to heal. Kastor deserved to pay for what he had done, but most importantly, I had to help my friends who had come for me. If Kastor won, he could turn the tide against them. My friends risked themselves in spite of my foolishness, and I couldn't let them suffer because of it.

The wound in my shoulder finished healing, and in the midst of the melee, I allowed myself a smile. I loved being a vampire.

"It's almost worth letting you live," I said. "Maimed like your boss and with the shame of having it done by one so young." I blocked a cut. "But not quite."

I renewed my focus and, with a few quick strikes, became the aggressor. One firm, precise swing after another left Kastor struggling to keep up. I stepped and cut and stepped and cut—*tyn!-tyn!*—*tyn!-tyn!*—our swords clashed. Working my way to where Zhilan fought Alexander and Silas, I pushed forward two or three steps for each single retreat my opponent caused.

I cut low—*tyn!*—Kastor met my blade.

I cut high—*tyn*—he met it, but he had gotten there late. My solid blow against his weak block sent his sword flying wide.

I slashed from his shoulder down diagonally—*fshwt*—blood gushed from his chest. He tried to hold it in with both hands. I stepped forward and to the side and swung at his neck. Kastor closed his eyes.

Fshwt!

His head fell to the floor in front of him.

Alexander stopped to watch his companion's body slump to the concrete. Victoria raced from her fight toward the one-armed vampire. Ariane followed a few steps behind and then came Caterine and Hayden. Victoria slashed down and had Alexander's arm off just as he finished turning to her.

She ducked under a swing from Ariane and thrust her blade into Alexander's stomach. Hayden arrived in time to block Caterine's strike at Victoria's back. Victoria lifted her blade up through Alexander's body and skull. Blood poured from Alexander's split head and body as they hit the ground. Victoria re-engaged with the twins.

With Zhilan one-on-one with Silas, I ran to help Grant, who had been slowed by a few bullets, and had the last four of Alexander's troops after him. I surprised one, leaving only three. Grant gunned down another, and the last two sped out of the room. Grant and I stopped to take a breath. Melted silver in his system was probably preventing his wounds from healing faster, but he had proven too tough to let it stop him.

Hayden had been bloodied, but he and Victoria appeared a reasonable match for the twins. Silas looked to be holding his own against Zhilan, but she didn't seem to be getting herself into any particularly dangerous situations.

Purple light filled the windows at the top of the walls. Almost all at once, the others found time to pause and notice the color. No one took advantage of the sudden break to launch back into an attack. We all knew what it meant.

Zhilan set an example by darting back to Grant and me. Silas didn't follow. He bowed slightly and ran out of the room. With flicks of her wrist, Ariane casually spun her katana at her side.

"I will kill you, Vera," Caterine called. "Or my sister will. I swear it."

Ariane stopped her spinning sword and smiled. The twins raced down the hall and out of sight.

Grant handed me his jacket, which I put on and zipped up.

Zhilan turned to me. "Co—"

Fshwt!

Victoria chopped off what remained of Alexander's head and kicked it away from his neck. With everyone watching—*crrrshhh*—she stepped on a big piece. She found another—*crrrshhh*—then another—*crrrshhh*. She replaced her sword on her back, brought her red cross necklace out from under her top, and kissed it. She took the scabbard for my sword off her back and gave it to me.

Victoria nodded at me. She and Zhilan exchanged a quick glance and nod, before Victoria sped out of the room.

"Come on," Zhilan said.

I put away my sword and motioned to the people chained to the walls. "What about them?"

"No time and no room," Grant said.

Zhilan grabbed my arm. "I'm sorry, Erin. We have to go."

She started to leave, and I ran along with her so she didn't have to drag me. We raced past the shot, sliced, and lifeless bodies of Alexander's gang members. Based on all I had seen come and go while captive, I suspected many others had fled. We passed the gate and Alexander's unarmed defenses. Half a mile away, we piled into a blue jeep that Max was driving. With every seat taken, and weapons and supplies filling the trunk, we made it to a safe house in a suburban development eight minutes later.

Shades of light blue and morning's first yellow crept over

the horizon by the time we pulled into the garage. We ran down to the basement where ten plain black coffins were neatly arranged.

"Take the one on the end," Zhilan said to me.

Another coffin. "I… I…"

Standing over a different one, Grant opened and closed its lid. "These don't lock. When you wake, push, and it'll open."

I walked slowly to where Zhilan had pointed and climbed in. I held the lid open. I was strong and free of that place, I assured myself.

With a deep breath, I lowered the lid until it closed. My hands clutched my sword scabbard on top of me. The night ended.

15

When I woke after sunset, at around six thirty, Zhilan had already gone, so I didn't get a chance to thank her. Grant, who had only partially healed during the day, told me that the night before, she had gotten a message from Victoria saying that I had been taken prisoner and that she was going after me. Apparently, when they had captured William, Alexander's vampires blabbed to him about me, and he told Victoria when he escaped. Victoria had informed Zhilan of her rescue attempt, in case it failed. If Zhilan and the others hadn't shown up, it very well could have.

I thanked Hayden, Grant, and Max profusely. Grant tried to apologize for not talking me out of going to Alexander's in the first place, but I wouldn't let him. For all of its horror, Alexander's had taught me lessons I might never had learned otherwise. Much to my relief, Grant had gotten to Carla a few nights after our meeting in Richmond. Her memory returned, as Sagar's had. By the time Sagar had been released, he had already decided to leave the Spectavi.

Once home, I still hadn't fed, but after doing so late the night before, I didn't feel like rushing to. The hunger paled in comparison to what I had endured while locked in that coffin. It wouldn't be pleasant, but contrary to my prior insistence, I did not have to feed every night.

I might also have simply been depressed. The excitement of my escape had faded, and under the hot water of my shower, I sat, bombarded by memory upon memory of my many mistakes.

After almost an hour, I went out to my back porch and sat in one of the simple chairs under the clear night sky. A high wooden fence surrounded my small yard. Almost right away, I went inside and grabbed a sofa cushion to rest my head on while lying on the concrete instead. I would have to buy better furniture for out there soon. Beyond that, looking up at the stars, trying to truly wrap my head around the idea that I could have an endless string of nights ahead of me, I didn't know what else to do.

I had been so foolish. I shuddered, remembering painful details from inside the steel coffin. My stupidity had rendered me caged, savage, and at the mercy of all of those monsters, and it could have been even worse. My immortal life had nearly been cut very short.

And while it hadn't, Todd's memory of me had been lost forever. I debated going after him anyway—eventually, when the time was right—but since he wouldn't know me, I wasn't sure it made sense. Maybe his new reality had become the best place for him. Once more, I cursed myself for rushing to attack Alexander.

At Eure, before freeing the twins, I had spent a long night going over all of my mistakes. As my anger built, I had dealt with it by counting down the hours until I would act.

As my fresh despair deepened, no clear goal lay ahead of me. I recalled all the people I had killed. Instead of searching for something in them that would have made me want to spare their lives, I should have found such a thing in myself. If I could have done that, ahead of time, I would only have had to do it once, not with every person, every night. All I had drunk from had lives that included both happiness and pain, and if I had accepted responsibility for letting them live, I could have enjoyed any of their memories, instead of seeking out their bleakest or doubting myself afterward when choosing not to.

But I hadn't understood that. Racing from one night to the next, I hadn't taken the time to let myself learn. I had hardly even considered all that had happened to me and what I had seen and chosen at death's door.

All at once, I pictured the pure white light, Mayumi, Kyle the crooked money manager, and the cross tattooed on my neck. 'Thou shalt not murder' was the commandment, but I didn't know. The world seemed better without those two. What more fitting way to mock Satan's evil than to use his power to remove such vile people from the earth?

My train of thought came to a screeching halt… then the machine slowly lurched forward. Edmond had killed indiscriminately. He sought to kill all the Sanguans, innocent or not. I had the power and finally the sense to choose to kill the wicked who crossed my path. Maybe it was one way to atone for taking so many good lives.

Of course, I would be robbing such people of a chance

to ask God for forgiveness of their sins. But I knew their minds and their feelings, and had found no hint of remorse in Kyle or Mayumi. Perhaps they would have changed later in life, but perhaps not.

As Grant had urged, I had decided how *I* valued human life. My cross would remind me that murdering God's innocent humans was wrong, but it would not tie me to a religious doctrine.

At the same time, all I had seen and done in the last few months reinforced my belief that a primitive battle between good and evil did rage on. I didn't understand it, but no longer human, I felt very close to that battle.

I had no answer for why God would let our demonic kind into the world, but he had. My power was real, and while I had to be more careful, I would use that power as I saw fit. Kyle and Mayumi had ruined lives and deserved to die. So had Edmond and Alexander. Christopher? I didn't regret killing him, either.

Around one a.m., I decided to get up from the concrete and replace my phone that had been left at Alexander's. At the mall a few blocks from my home, as soon as the store clerk linked my new one to my account, a text read:

It's Victoria. Text me when you get this. We should meet.

It didn't seem unreasonable that someone in her position would be able to track me down, but it did strike me as odd to read a text from someone born in the twelfth century. Immediately upon leaving the store, I texted: *Meet tonight?*

She responded before I got home. *Top of Pentagon City Mall parking garage in an hour?*

I sent *Yes*, and saved her as a new contact before turning around and heading back to the mall.

––––––––––––

Past a low concrete wall, a highway ran between me and the Pentagon. Farther in the distance, the Washington Monument and Capitol were illuminated. A soft wind blew, and a crescent moon gave little light. Jeans were nice for a change, and my hands found homes in my coat pockets while I waited.

"Vera," Victoria called. "You named it Tomori."

She had arrived behind me, walking between the few remaining cars parked in the lot. She wore pants for the first time I had ever seen. More typically, they were worn leather, and so was her long coat. Like me, she appeared unarmed. Her long hair was loose and occasionally blew over the cold, uncaring face I had seen so many times at Eure.

As she came closer, I noticed the absence of a sterile smell that I hadn't paid attention to in the past. Her allegiance clearly lay with the Spectavi, but like Edmond, she must not have drunk their synthetic creation.

"Your sword was forged in 1438, and when I gave it to you on your thirteenth birthday, you named it Tomori, after 'Memento mori,' a Latin phrase meaning, 'Remember you must die.' *Memento mori* is a type of art intended to remind us all of our mortality. You were in a dark place then, but I did think it was a clever name for a sword." A hint of warmth in her face revealed itself when she got close, and the same comfort I had felt at Alexander's began to return. She had seemed such a monster, and had lived up to the word by nearly killing me. Since she had rescued me, I no longer feared she wanted to hurt me, but still didn't understand her.

"What changed since Edmond's basement?" I asked.

A slight smile brightened her face further. "I was wrong. When you were gone from that basement, along with Edmond's blood, I knew I had been wrong about you. Edmond's misguided attempt to help you hadn't fully driven your strength from you. He pushed you to the brink, and when I could no longer stand what you had become, I tried to push you over it. But you didn't break. You pushed back and survived."

She became serious. "I will miss Edmond, but he deserved his fate. And through his death, you became a vampire like I always hoped you would. Night after night, I watched you grow up, and it was a selfish wish because you steadfastly refused. But I didn't want to see you grow old. You were such a strong young woman. I never wanted to have to see you die."

Tears welled in my eyes for the life I couldn't remember.

Victoria crossed her arms. "And then, when your image started showing up on building security cameras near murders all over the area, I knew you had become reckless, as well. It was hardly shocking, after all you had been through, but know that without my intervention, you would have been a hunted criminal. I am here to tell you, that intervention ends tonight. You need to be far more careful."

"I'm sorry." I stared at the parking space lines, ashamed.

"And when word reached me that you had attacked

Alexander, and failed, I knew your recklessness had gone too far. Sofie, a fledgling of mine that Alexander killed, was much older than you when he defeated her. You are so very young."

I continued to stare down. "I wanted to be a lion." It sounded pitiful. "I was such a weak girl. I didn't want to be weak anymore."

"So *be* a lion." Victoria's face lit up completely, inviting me back to it. "Be strong, decisive, and courageous, but don't be reckless. A reckless lion wouldn't survive in the jungle, just as a reckless vampire will not survive out here." Victoria stepped forward and grasped my arms with her white hands. "Control the lion. Don't let the lion control you."

I had learned the lesson at Alexander's, and remembered it, alone at my house. All I could do was nod, while Victoria's touch and words drove it to my core.

"Good." Victoria stepped back. "Good. Thank you for meeting me tonight. I have to go, but I am sure I will see you again soon."

"Thank you for rescuing me," I said.

"You're welcome."

She started to leave, and I struggled to remember the questions I had come up with on the way over. After hardly considering all that remained unanswered about Vera, I couldn't waste the opportunity. "What happened to my human parents? Are they still alive?"

Victoria turned back. "No, they are not alive. It is a sad story, and one for another time."

"Please tell me," I pleaded.

She looked up at the sky, then checked her phone. She walked to the end of the lot and motioned to the ledge. Her long coat ran down behind her when she sat with her legs dangling over the wall's edge. I joined her just to her left, feeling like a child compared to the larger, ancient vampire.

"Edmond and I never met your parents." Victoria gazed toward the Pentagon across from us, while starting out with that major disappointment. "But we did learn all about them when you came to us. Eventually, we read your memories, and before that, we talked to many of their friends and co-workers. I have seen enough over my long life that I believe I came to understand your parents very well."

That sounded more hopeful.

Victoria continued, "You were born in 1987 and—"

"What day?"

She turned to me momentarily. "January seventh."

At least Edmond had given me my actual birthday. I really was twenty-two… and I always would be.

"Your parents were close to graduating high school when your mother became pregnant. Their friends said that neither had been a great student, and when they fell in love, it only made them less interested in school. You were unexpected, but neither had aspirations for college, anyway.

"You were born Vera Clarke in Fairfax, Virginia. Your mother, Emily Moretti, of Italian descent, raised you, while your father, Ryan—he was Irish—got a job as a construction worker. The job paid well, and he proved good at it. When you were five and started going to school, your mother took shifts as a cashier at a local grocery store. Those early years were happy ones for your family."

Every word from Victoria was a gift I had feared would never come. I wanted her to slow down and give much greater detail, just as I wished she would hurry up and reveal the ending.

"You had always seemed smart to your parents, but until you went to kindergarten, you didn't really make it clear just how far ahead of your classmates you were. You brought home children's books from school but set them aside to read the newspaper. You finished your counting and basic math worksheets, then solved the puzzles in the paper that your parents couldn't figure out themselves.

"Before the end of first grade, you were in advanced classes with fourth and fifth graders. By second grade, those classes weren't useful to you any longer, but the school district deemed you too young to take classes with any older students. Their suggestion was a private school for gifted children, but your parents couldn't afford it. Emily's parents had no money to spare. Ryan's might have, but he refused to ask them.

"For two years, you stayed in public school, and Ryan's refusal to ask his parents for money became a constant source of tension between your parents. Their friends said they had never seen the two of them so unhappy as a couple.

"Then when you were nine, your father got a promotion, and with your mother working extra shifts, they were able to send you to the better school. From your first day there, you loved it and soaked up information like a sponge. Math, science, history, literature—you name it, you excelled at it. Your family was happy again.

"One day, Edmond visited the school, as he did from time to time to meet with some of the older students. He liked to take a personal role in recruiting the best and the brightest for Eure. When Edmond passed you in the hallway and asked how you were doing, you said, 'Bad.' He asked why, and the two of you launched into an hour-long discussion about the President's State of the Union speech from the night before. You disagreed with much of it.

"Edmond mentioned you to me the next time I saw him. He said he looked forward to when you were older, and hoped you would want to join us at Eure. After that, for about a year, you continued to love school, and all was well."

Victoria glanced over and smiled when she found me completely enthralled. The smile morphed into a sad grimace. "Unfortunately, when you were ten, your father was killed trying to break up a bar fight between co-workers. Four men beat him to death. Worse, because he hadn't died at work and had drunk one beer too many, the life insurance company wouldn't pay his policy.

"You and your mother were crushed. So were Ryan's parents. And they wanted to help keep sending you to the private school, but your grandmother had become very ill, so their finances had become strained. What money they could give you went to pay basic expenses for you and your mother.

"You put on a brave face, assured everyone you were happy to have their love and support, and went back to public school. Your mother hated that you had to, but with no career beyond the grocery store, she couldn't do anything about it. Every day, she prayed for some small miracle that would allow you to return to the better school.

"One night, late at work, a Sanguan came in and asked your mother if she would let him bite her. She said no. He asked if he could pay to drink from her. Again, she refused. The vampire left his phone number and moved on."

Victoria gave me another sad look. "After thinking it over for two days, your mother decided that the Sanguan had been the answer to her prayers. She called him and met him. Once he had drunk from her, she asked for an advance on his payments. He agreed, and meeting him twice a week, she was able to pay for you to go back to the private school.

"She told you that one of her friends had lent her the money, but that you couldn't thank him because his wife wouldn't understand. As excited as you were, that explanation and condition were fine with you.

"For almost a year, you were happy at school, while your mother became weaker and weaker, as Bernard took more blood. She assured you that it was simply the effects of her long hours at work, so she wouldn't miss a loan payment to her friend. Every day, you told her how much you loved her for working so hard for you.

"One day, when you were eleven, your mother didn't come home after you thought she had been at work. Her body was found two days later. Bernard had taken too much.

"Your father's father, Jack, came to stay with you, but his wife's condition had grown worse, and he didn't think he could care for you for very long. You understood and didn't want to put such a burden on him. Your mother's parents wouldn't take you in, and their home wasn't a very happy one anyway. That meant a foster home and public school. You had another idea.

"You took a taxi to Eure headquarters and demanded to see Edmond. The vampire at the gate refused and told the cab to turn around. You got out and sent the taxi away. The guard still wouldn't let you pass, and he called the police. When they arrived, you wouldn't tell them who you were, so they called Social Services. You kicked and screamed as you were dragged into the social worker's car.

"When the car started driving away, you opened the door and leapt out. The guard raced to see if you were hurt. You weren't, aside from a few scrapes, and you demanded again to see Edmond. This time, he agreed to take your name and ask if Edmond was willing to see you. Edmond said yes.

"When you told Edmond what had happened, he arranged for you to stay with us. Your grandfather signed over your custody when you assured him it was what you wanted, and he concluded that doing so gave you the best chance to reach the great potential you showed. From then on, you lived at Eure, and Edmond and I raised you."

I wiped away a tear and spent a few seconds trying to process it all. "What happened to Bernard?"

"Edmond killed him a few months later."

"What about my grandparents?"

Victoria stared straight ahead, as if recalling the facts. "Last I checked, a year ago, your mother's parents were alive, but had divorced. Your father's mother passed away. His father is still alive."

"When did Edmond first drink from me?"

"When you were fifteen, after you begged him to do it for over a year."

"And you?"

"After that."

I nodded.

"I'm sorry about your parents, Vera," Victoria said. "By all accounts, they loved you more than anything in the world."

Tears ran down my cheeks.

Victoria placed her hand on my shoulder. "They would be proud of you. Over eight hundred years, I've seen one cruel twist of fate after another. I've watched men, women, and vampires wilt and surrender in the face of life's challenges, resigning themselves to what they feel is inevitable or impossible to overcome. You've never surrendered. You've always fought for what you wanted."

I grew ashamed once more. "I gave up at Alexander's."

"No, you did not. You are still here."

My head went to her shoulder, and she held me, saying, "I'm sorry I let Edmond do what he did to you. I should have stopped him."

I wept for my lost parents, and once again, for my lost life. Why hadn't she stopped him? Everything could have been so different. At the same time, hearing the story of my parents was like having a locked door finally ripped open. Some of my tears were tears of joy. But most came from recalling the many lows of the last two years. The excruciating pain of not knowing had been so hard. Eventually, I forced myself to stop crying, and leaned away from Victoria. I wiped my face with my hand and sleeve.

"What will you do now?" she asked

I pictured the lion. After all Victoria had said, it didn't sound so pitiful. It sounded like something young Vera would have fought for. "I'll beg Zhilan to forgive me and to teach me. I have a lot to learn, about everything."

"Don't beg," Victoria said. "Zhilan has made her mistakes. She stood idle while Sofie was tortured before Alexander killed her. Remind her of that if you have to, but don't beg."

"All right. Why did you wait so long to go after him?"

"We tried, from time to time. But it often went badly, and he always fled. Edmond hated losing so many vampires, considering the multitude of other targets, so Alexander became a lower priority. This time, I think he put too much faith in Edmond's sisters, so he stuck around."

I nodded. "What will you do?"

Weariness flashed over Victoria's face. "The twins must be captured or, now that Edmond is gone, killed. I don't know what their next move will be, but I will have to answer it."

"I'm so sorry for letting them loose."

"It wasn't your fault. It was Edmond's. They've sworn to kill both of us now."

"They won't." Adrenaline shot through me.

"No." Pride mixed in with Victoria's weariness. "Erin…"

It obviously strained her to say the name, but her face relaxed after getting it out for the first time. "Erin, be strong and be brave, but be smarter. Be beautiful and be powerful. Become the vampire I always hoped you would."

With that, she jumped down from the ledge and sped away.

Brring......brring......brring......brring......brring......brr ing.

The call ended. It was only eight thirty, but maybe already too late. Or Victoria could have texted me the wrong number.

I doubted she would have, so I hit redial.

Brring...brring...

"Hello?" an old man's voice answered.

"Mr. Clarke?"

"Yes."

I froze.

"Yes," he said again. "Hello?"

"Jack Clarke?"

"Yes, who is this? What do you want?"

I had to say it. "It's Vera."

"Vera?" He sounded shocked.

"Yes... Vera Clarke. Your... granddaughter."

"Vera," he said softly. "My God."

I pulled into the driveway at my grandfather's house in Manassas, Virginia, and turned off Zhilan's Mercedes.

Convincing Zhilan that I understood she had been right hadn't taken much more than showing up at her house after Victoria had left. Zhilan had apologized for trying to force her point of views on me so quickly. I explained to her that the sum of all that had happened was what taught me.

Zhilan and I discussed what Victoria had revealed to me, and what to do about it. If Zhilan had counseled waiting to see my grandfather, I would have. I think her hearing that, and seeing how the story weighed on me and distracted me, led her to urge me to call my grandfather. Victoria's words had sounded so genuine, but I had fallen in that trap before with Edmond. I had to know for sure.

I got out and shut the car door. A porch light illuminated the brown door of the one-story house. My drive had taken me past numerous new developments, but my grandfather's was an older one. His lawn and shrubs had been recently cut.

When I had made it halfway up the concrete path, the door opened.

"Erin." The large, Irish man in a navy sweater, with a head full of silver hair smiled warmly.

"Grandpa…" I started.

"It's all right. I told you, you can call me Jack." He opened the screen all the way, and I went inside. At fifty-eight, he was still tall, and it seemed a reasonable bet that my father had been, as well.

He stood on a small mat at the entrance, and his green eyes met mine. "You're all grown up," he said, choking up a little. He recovered and added, "I was so worried about you, but you're fine. You're all grown up."

On the phone earlier, after explaining some of what had happened to me, my grandfather revealed that he hadn't seen me in seven years and that I hadn't called in over four. He had tried to contact me, but I never picked up or responded to his messages. He assumed I had moved on with my life, with the vampires I had been so happy with, and didn't want anything else to do with him. I apologized, but he wouldn't accept it, and instead offered his own regret for not trying harder to find out what was going on with me at Eure. I begged him not to feel guilty and guessed that perhaps I had stopped returning his calls after getting wrapped up in my scientific work.

My grandfather headed through a short hallway to a kitchen. We passed pictures of people I assumed were my grandmother, my father, my mother… and me. I stopped and leaned to look closely at a picture of a young girl standing across from her parents, eating a vanilla ice cream cone.

My grandfather looked at the picture over my shoulder. "That's you. You loved your ice cream."

I would have rushed to taste a scoop as soon as I left there, if only I could. I made sure to smile so he wouldn't catch my disappointment.

"Have a seat," he said, motioning into the kitchen at a circular wooden table. A yellow dome light hung above it.

I sat at one of the three wooden chairs that were perfectly positioned around the table. Jack took the one chair that was askew. I started off with one of the few things I was certain of wanting to say. "Thanks for seeing me on such short notice, and so late."

He waved his hand. "Of course. Thank you for calling me and coming out here." He pushed up the sleeve of his sweater. "Why wait? Talking will be more productive after than before."

I grew intensely nervous. Zhilan had said that drinking from a relative could be very emotional. She had also explained that it was the act of extracting blood that let us read people's thoughts, not merely the blood itself. I couldn't simply swallow a vial of my grandfather's blood that had been drawn by a needle.

I reminded myself that Zhilan trusted I could handle the situation, or she would have told me not to go. I had practiced drinking in short spurts at Cain's. Aside from the confidence it gave me for my grandfather, it encouraged me to be in greater control of myself when feeding. I had drunk plenty before the trip to Manassas.

Looking down at his pale wrist, I imagined how different it would be. The visions when the first drop hit me would be an experience more personal than any bite that had come before. I scooted my chair closer and took his upturned forearm in my right hand and his palm in my left. I glanced at the first family member I could ever remember touching. He nodded reassuringly.

Slowly, I brought his wrist up and leaned down at the same time. Resting my fangs on his skin, I couldn't ignore the strong beats of his old heart. I closed my eyes.

Warm blood…

Fire!

Victoria had told the truth. I stopped drinking.

My grandfather's eyes had opened by the time mine were, if they had ever closed. "That wasn't so bad," he said.

I let go of his wrist and wiped the first tear from my eye. "No." I sniffled and tried to force a smile. There was so much more to see, but that breathtaking sip had shown me so much already.

Through my grandfather's eyes, I had seen my young mother the first day she came home with my father. She had been so beautiful. My father glowed while introducing his new girlfriend. My grandfather saw how happy his son was with her in his life.

I watched my parents' small wedding, after their senior year of high school, where my mother's white dress hung over her round belly.

I glimpsed myself as a baby in the hospital, minutes into my life.

When I was a little older, my grandfather loved for me to sit on his lap and read to him. When he visited, he bought me ice cream and candy, even when my grandmother told him I had enough. He didn't care to listen to her. He couldn't do anything extravagant, so he'd spoil his only granddaughter with little treats. He knew Grandma didn't *really* care.

I saw my grandmother grow sick, and the doctor describing the cancer they could do nothing to stop. I caught images of Grandma holding on, her body slowly failing for years, until she passed away.

I saw my father visit his sick mother, sometimes with me, sometimes without, until the day he had been killed in that bar fight.

I witnessed my grandparents argue over the money they could afford to give my mother to help support her and me. They gave all they could, but wished they could have given much more.

I understood the hatred my grandfather had held for the men who had killed his good son, and knew his resentment for a god that would let his beloved wife get so sick. I felt his relief when he forgave the men who had repented and the god who he believed had to have a plan for everything. He missed his wife, but had learned to focus on the time they had, not that the chance for more had been taken away.

I felt my grandfather's sorrow when my mother died and he couldn't support me, just as I felt his tremendous hope and pride when he had met Edmond and Victoria. The ancient, virtuous vampires had considered me worthy of being among them, and I had sworn over and over to my grandfather my desire to go. My grandfather realized that with the Spectavi, doors would open for me that might never otherwise, even if my parents had still been alive. He saw God's hand at work.

He knew that with the Spectavi, I might become a vampire one day and live forever. When I walked in, a small part of him wished that Vera the vampire had walked in instead. But he had grown too overjoyed seeing me to continue caring who I had become, and found faith that God had a plan for Erin Rose. Then we sat down, and then I bit his wrist.

"It's a lot all at once," I said. My grandfather got up and came back with a tissue for me. "Thanks." I took it and blew my nose.

"I hope you're right, and God does have a plan for me."

I had caught my grandfather off guard by responding to something he had never actually mentioned to me out loud.

"I truly believe He does," he said, when he figured it out. He shrugged. "But no matter what, there's nothing for you to do but live your life. You must have seen a great deal of sadness in my blood, but you should have seen plenty of joy as well. Dwelling on my pain, hating God, and then pleading to him for answers got me nowhere. One day, I woke up and decided to try to remember only the good times in my long life. It's a struggle, like everything, but my days have been happier ever since."

He placed his hand over mine on the table. "You've been through a lot, and now you've seen some of it for yourself. But don't dwell on it. You're young and have been given such a gift to have forever ahead of you. Don't waste it looking back. Drink from me again, if you want to remember more, but let those visits be only brief breaks from a new life you're forging ahead with."

We spoke for hours, but had already gotten to the heart of the matter. Victoria had told the truth, and I had just seen a portion of my past with greater depth and feeling than any photographs or videos could ever have shown. My grandfather told story after story, and I had taken so little blood, so quickly, that many of the details in each were new to me. He made sure to steer each tale to an upbeat conclusion and reiterated over and over that the point of reminiscing wasn't to end up sad, but to put ourselves once more in the joyous moments of our lives.

I felt more complete than ever as Erin. Finally, I had glimpses of my own life to look back on. It was a fraction of the lost emotion, and it would come from an external point of view, but it was infinitely more than a blank slate.

I was also thankful to have another vampire in the world to learn from. Victoria hadn't apologized for nearly killing me, but she had given me a part of my life back. Coming to rescue me was a good start in regaining my trust, and leading me to my grandfather was another big step.

When it had gotten late, I confessed some of my horrible mistakes since becoming a vampire. My grandfather implored me to learn from them and to do better. By that point, I couldn't have imagined him saying anything else.

An hour before sunrise, I left his home, so thankful to have survived Alexander's to have had the meeting. I also left with the promises that I would return before long, and that I wouldn't let my new life be weighed down by the sorrow that filled both of our pasts.

I spent the first few hours of the following night on my back porch, staring up at the sky, doing exactly what I had promised not to do. My parents had both been tall. My father's green eyes, which had come from his parents, had made it all the way down to me. My mother's long brown hair was a touch darker than my chestnut. Everything had gone so wrong for them.

Then I remembered my parents together—their visible love for each other and for me. I replayed those scenes over and over, and all the sad ones less and less. Eventually, I had seen enough of the good moments and didn't want to go back to the others. I went to Zhilan's, and she politely asked how everything had gone with my grandfather. I told her about it, then asked if we could spar.

The rate of our sword strokes built as the night wore on. At first, I fought like I had before in her basement. Then, recalling my duel with Kastor and how I had defeated him, I began to move faster. With wooden crack upon wooden crack, our contest progressed to a whole new level.

Hour after hour, I raced around the basement with an energy and a purpose I had never fought with before. Memories of my family propelled me. I battled against their hardships, relished their joy, and swore to be deserving of all they had done for me. Unlike any other night we had practiced, I sensed Zhilan summoning her own emotion to keep up and fight back. She understood exactly what her young opponent needed.

16

Sparring with Zhilan had energized me. I had made so many mistakes, but wallowing in self-pity would have been another one. My grandfather had told me that, and Zhilan couldn't help subtly offering the same suggestion. Most importantly, *I* believed it.

The pain and horror of Alexander's would take time to fade, but it would fade, and Alexander would remain dead. The same would hold true for Eure and Edmond. I considered myself very lucky to have survived both places. Whatever fate or bad luck beyond my control had led to the life of Erin Rose, my own poor choices had almost led to its end.

It was tremendously satisfying to finally know where I had come from, and to have some memories of that past. It also gave me a fresh perspective. My life *had* been very hard, but so had my parents' and my grandparents'. The world itself was hard, but opportunity lay before me. It was time to learn how to live right.

Zhilan and I trained for three nights. Based on what Victoria had said and the markings on the sword, Zhilan told me of the vampire who had created Tomori and what a priceless weapon it was. She agreed with Victoria that I had chosen a good name for it.

We continued to spar with bokken because Zhilan said steel would always be dangerous. I didn't complain. We also practiced more without weapons, so I would be better prepared for something like what had led to my capture. Zhilan did not have to convince me of the value of those lessons.

We were taking the night off, and she promised not to follow me after the short meeting we were attending. She said it was a relief that she could get back to her own life for a change, but I suspected a part of her would have preferred to continue keeping close tabs on me.

Twenty minutes outside Washington, halfway to Annapolis, Maryland, Zhilan parked her car in a suburban driveway. "The bond is stronger the longer you have drunk, and the hunger you will both feel is proportionately powerful. It should not surprise you that the price of such an enjoyable experience must be paid with even more human blood."

"It doesn't." I got out and closed the door. Zhilan had answered my question about vampires drinking from vampires. As awful as it had been when Alexander sucked the life out of me, drinking from Christopher had been incredible. Having seen two vampires at each other's necks before, I wondered why I didn't see it all the time.

According to Zhilan, the experience could be amazing, but there were downsides. For one, two vampires couldn't live merely by drinking from each other. If one started in need of blood, and took more than they gave, the other would be left hungry. In that case, human blood was the only way to leave both vampires fulfilled.

Assuming two vampires were well fed at the start, when they were done, the "bond" Zhilan had mentioned meant a bond in hunger. Based on how long they had fed from one another, each vampire would awaken the following night to an increased thirst, and share that thirst with their partner. For each, it would be worse and harder to satisfy than usual. Very old vampires, who didn't normally have to feed often, would usually have to in that case.

"Don't get me wrong," Zhilan said as we neared the door of the small house. "It is yet another sublime gift to be a vampire and mix blood with another, but the resulting thirst will be intense and can leave you vulnerable. If your partner has not fed, or something happens to them and they cannot feed, as their pain grows, it can also be agony for you."

A vampire in a black suit opened the door. Walking through another barren house, Zhilan and I joined Hayden and Houjin, and sat down at the kitchen table.

Grant came in the front door. "You drive like a madwoman!"

Zhilan smiled. "If you and your little bike cannot keep up, it is not my problem."

"It's not a little bike." Grant sat down.

Houjin let a smile fade and spoke up. "Erin, we are glad you are still with us."

"Me too," I said.

"Do you know why I did not accompany these three in your rescue?" he asked.

I shook my head.

"Aside from my disdain of personal quests for revenge, I deemed it an unacceptable risk for the life of one young vampire. I hope you have thanked those who judged otherwise."

The serious nature of the conversation was unexpected, but I truly hoped to keep my spot at the table with my friends, even if Houjin couldn't be counted among them. "I have thanked them. And I will again. I... acted foolishly. I'm sorry. I shouldn't have gone in the first place. I shouldn't have attacked Alexander. I shouldn't have done a lot of things. I finally understand that I have a lot to learn."

Houjin nodded. "I trust you have come to understand that, in part because your path reminds me of that which one of my own took. She turned out fine, except for the driving, apparently."

"Thank you!" Grant slapped his palm on the table.

Zhilan threw up her hands. "It's a sports car. I am not apologizing. In fact, I am driving my Ferrari next time you are following me."

"All right. All right," Houjin said. "Hayden, please go ahead."

Hayden got straight to it. "Caterine and Ariane are in Europe. France, England, Germany, and Italy for sure so far. Likely other countries, as well."

"What are they doing there?" Grant asked.

Hayden shook his head. "Hard to say. Some Spectavi

have been killed, and some people, but it's all been minor so far. If I had to guess, I'd say they were building up a network of loyal followers as they move, reconnecting with old vampires and revealing themselves to new ones. It's a logical step."

"I agree," Houjin said. "The war is changing. Alliances were broken at Alexander's compound."

"I'm sorry," I said again.

I felt so tiny, but Houjin didn't let it last. "Do not be sorry about that. Once Alexander placed himself in league with the twins, we could no longer be allied with him. The Spectavi are also changing. Reinald will lead them with the same goal as Edmond—to rid the world of blood-drinking vampires who aren't among the few ruling Spectavi—but his motivations will be different. Edmond was driven in part by dreams of healing his sisters and clearing his family name for starting all of this. I do not think Reinald will see any reason to keep the twins alive, if he can catch them, that is."

"I fear what they'll become," Grant said. "I don't know that this century can handle it."

Zhilan chimed in, "They aren't exactly invading Eden."

"True." Houjin rubbed his chin. "There are plenty of threats in the world, and these sisters, evil as they are, are just the latest. Still, they have been awakened at a time when our situation is quite dire. We needed something to change, and the two of them could change everything."

Grant leaned forward. "So we use them? I don't think we can control them."

"Not control," Houjin said. "For now, we can watch

them with a purpose. I've been thinking over what Erin and Grant discovered about the Spectavi synthetic. If we are ever again to live in a world where some Sanguans can exist peacefully, the Spectavi cannot remain as influential as they are now. Human governments might not tolerate the fabricated Spectavi justifications for why they hunt us, if they knew how the synthetic was really being used."

"So we tell the twins what's going on?" Hayden asked.

Zhilan spoke up. "They already know. Alexander would have told them."

Houjin pointed at her. "Correct. Synthetic blood is such a significant development that I do not think they will be able to ignore it. I expect them to realize how much more damaging to the Spectavi exposing its true nature could be than merely destroying it. While the two of them enjoy appearing wild and aggressive, they can also be as shrewd as Edmond. With the attention they are getting, they could generate enough outrage to fracture the human-Spectavi relationship."

"Do we push them in that direction?" Hayden asked.

"Not yet," Houjin said. "I believe they will get there themselves, and I do not want to risk having them alter their strategy to spite Sanguans like us."

"I'll make sure the others in Europe know," Hayden said.

Houjin nodded. "And I'll be sure that course and goal are understood among our allies here." He looked over the four of us. "This is not the first time our side of this war has splintered into more and less extreme factions, but it is the first time in hundreds of years. We can all hope that the circumstances of this century lead to the peace we have been fighting for, but we must also know that things need not end so well for any of us, or any humans. These times demand informed, deliberate strategy."

Houjin stood up. "Erin, you have my trust because you have Zhilan's. You may also have my praise. Besting Kastor was impressive, and we are lucky to have you and your sword on our side. Continue living up to the potential these three see in you, and next time you make a mistake, perhaps I will join them in coming to fetch you."

With that, Houjin walked out of the kitchen and out the front door. Hayden followed and then Grant, Zhilan, and I did. A black limousine drove Houjin away. Hayden's old Ford Mustang peeled out next.

I couldn't help calling to Grant while getting back into Zhilan's car. "Would you rather I drive, so you can keep up? Or do you just want to come with us?"

He pulled up to my lowered window. "I'm starting to think Houjin had the right idea to sit out your rescue."

Zhilan's acceleration pinned me to my seat when she sped off before Grant did.

After Zhilan dropped me back home, I changed and headed out to my last night in D.C. for a while. Ironically, all the moving pieces in the war had created a window of time for Zhilan, Grant, and I to travel. At least for the three of us, watching and planning seemed more important than active involvement at that moment.

The next night, we were going to New York City, where I had never been. From there, we would head west. Eventually, we might make it out of the U.S. for my first time ever. We'd spar some nights on the road and meet with vampires in other cities, but the highest priority was for me to live something of a 'normal' life, before circumstances dictated otherwise.

I anticipated growing restless occasionally, especially if news broke of Caterine and Ariane. Whether they came after me or not, they remained a massive loose end I considered myself responsible for. Hearing Victoria pin the blame on Edmond didn't change the fact that I was the one who had cut the tubes running to their coffins.

Even so, taking things a bit easier definitely appealed to me. I had spent almost every moment of my mortal life trying to solve a mystery, and all of my time as a vampire bent on revenge. Traveling and merely living life for a while didn't sound bad at all. As Zhilan had said, the war would be waiting for me after I had.

Zhilan suggested I read and shared her favorite way to experience books. She said that as an immortal, it would be silly not to take the time to travel to the settings of stories to really get into them. Reading had never been my favorite diversion, but the way she explained it, I looked forward to giving it a try. I also intended to pick up some non-fiction— perhaps history and science for starters—to see if my appetite and aptitude for learning came back.

I understood that books were a device to help calm me, but I didn't resent it. Happily, Zhilan had expressed no reservations about my less relaxed plans for the evening—seeing Shattered Nights. Their show was just about finished.

Piano notes of my favorite song carried across the largest club they had ever played. Luke's leather pants and white shirt looked good. I glanced at my leather pants and black tank top. My short hair still felt weird, but I had gotten it cleaned up since Alexander's. I looked good, too.

Luke sang, and the captivated crowd calmly danced along. From near the wall on the side, I did the same.

My eyes closed while the notes rose and fell. Gwen's bass beats hit perfectly. I was so thankful to have lived to hear their music again.

Luke sang louder and stood up from his bench, sweaty as always. His voice filled the big room completely. I loved that voice.

He played the long, last note.

Their love still burns.

Everyone cheered wildly, but I didn't join them.

"Thank you! Thank you all," Luke called out. After a few last beats, drumsticks flew out to eager recipients. The band walked off stage.

I raced from the crowd, out of the building and then around it. When I pulled open the back door, the band members inside faced away from me. I sped in, snatched Luke, and brought him outside. I slammed him against the closing steel door, then wrapped my hands around his biceps to hold him there. I leaned into his tense body. I had imagined the scene so many times, but couldn't afford to savor the moment any longer.

My forehead pushed aside a little of his long hair before my fangs pierced his salty, wet neck. His body relaxed. I sucked and grew warm, and then even warmer as his blood streamed into my mouth. Gulp after gulp, it raced over my tongue, down my throat. As my body grew hot all over, I wished to have been able to slow down and more thoroughly enjoy the sensation.

Boom! Boom! Boom! Bursts of flame hit like cannon fire.

People on the inside of the door pushed to open it. I pressed myself harder into Luke to push back, squeezed his arms tighter, then drove my fangs deeper and sucked out more blood.

Boom!

I watched his band celebrate their last show, and the one before that. I saw Gwen's disbelief when Luke broke up with her last year, and then pleaded with her to stay with the group.

Boom!

The blaze roared through me. Finally, Luke was its cause.

He had seen a woman run down to find a man drinking alone at a basement bar. I felt what Luke had felt, watching their tear-filled embrace, and then turning it into *Ember*. He wrote the first draft of lyrics on a white napkin, with the bartender's blue pen.

Boom! I drank on and had to know it all. I had to feel it all!

But I stopped and raised my fangs out of him.

Luke opened his eyes, and I let him go.

He took a short breath. "I wondered if you'd ever do it."

He grabbed me by my arms and spun us around. The door cracked open behind me. He pressed me back into it much more gently than I had with him and held me tightly there.

I pushed back myself to help keep the door closed. "What do you mean?"

"Your hair's shorter. I've seen you at some of our shows, standing like a statue in the back. I wondered what you wanted, and now I know."

Over all the nights I had considered drinking from him, of all the reactions I had imagined him having, that one was among my wildest fantasies.

"Take more," Luke said. He inched his neck closer.

I heard faint sirens as I leaned into him and, without breaking the skin, tapped my fangs just above where I had bitten.

I kissed his cheek, then whispered, "I will."

THE END OF BOOK III

CONNECT ONLINE

Thanks for reading. If you enjoyed the story, please leave a review at your favorite online retailer.

Get the latest updates about S.M. Perlow's works by signing up for his newsletter:

smperlow.com/newsletter

Find him online at:

smperlow.com

twitter.com/smperlow

facebook.com/smperlow

Works by S.M. Perlow

Vampires and the Life of Erin Rose

Novels
Choosing a Master
Alone
Lion
Hope
War

Short Stories
Alice Stood Up

—

The Grand Crucible

Novels
Golden Dragons, Gilded Age

—

Other Works

Short Stories
The Girl Who Was Always Single

www.ingramcontent.com/pod-product-compliance
Lightning Source LLC
Chambersburg PA
CBHW021004120726
47905CB00009B/2853